DEADLY HIDEAWAY

A
GEORGIA RAE WINSTON
MYSTERY

MARISSA SHROCK

CIMELIAPRESS

Published by Cimelia Press, Greentown, Indiana

Printed in the United States of America

Print ISBN-13: 978-0-9969879-6-7

Library of Congress Control Number: 2020908240

Trust in him at all times, you people; pour out your hearts to him, for God is our refuge.

Psalm 62:8

AUTHOR'S NOTE

As with the previous books in this series, I took some geographical liberties with Indiana and created some new places. Georgia's home of Wildcat Springs is a fictional town in Central Indiana, and Hidden Shores, Lake Hideaway, and Webster County in Northern Indiana are all products of my imagination.

However, Lake Hideaway has some intentional similarities to Lake Wawasee, which is Indiana's largest natural lake. I have many fond memories of spending time there every summer for the last thirty years.

Finally, I also used some fictional license with police procedures to maintain the pace and flow of the story.

CHAPTER ONE

Lake Hideaway had always been a perfect place to—well—hide away, and the status of my ever-chaotic love life demanded that I escape to a safe haven.

On a sweltering July evening, I was singing along with the Brooklyn Tabernacle Choir while driving my truck on the curvy, tree-lined road that looped the Northern Indiana lake. I spotted water shimmering between the colorful cottages on the vast western shore.

Okay, so most of the cottages were actually million-dollar mansions.

As if he sensed my anticipation over a much-needed vacation, my yellow Labrador retriever Gus wiggled in my truck's passenger seat, and the window displayed his streaky, nose-print art.

"Almost there, Gus."

He panted and thumped his tail against the seat.

Spotting a brick sign, I turned in to Hideaway Acres. My friend Laura's new home was located in this subdivision full of houses built along a channel that was a short ride to the lake. The quiet street circled a large common area with a playground and picnic benches. A few kids were swinging and zipping down the red curly slide.

Laura had warned me she wouldn't be home when I arrived but had told me I could get a key from the lady in the yellow house next door. I parked in Laura's driveway, and as I shut off my truck, I eyed her two-story brick house that'd been painted a soft gray. Her front porch held an American flag and a hanging basket of purple and pink petunias.

"Nice place, Gus."

He shimmied in response, and I figured he needed to relieve himself. Not only had it been a long ride, but I'd also stopped at a McDonald's drive through, and Gus might or might not have stolen a couple of my French fries.

I hooked his leash to his collar, and we got out. Even though it was well past seven, humidity lingered, and the sounds of giggling children punctuated the breeze. While Gus sniffed around the yard, I surveyed the neighborhood.

A cottage with dark blue shake siding and a patriotic bunting hanging from the porch stood to the east. The neighbor's house to the west was painted a buttery yellow, and the landscaping boasted an elaborate variety of flowers and cheerful garden gnomes. An open garage door displayed a black Explorer and a motorcycle.

The high-pitched whine of an ice cream truck blasting "Do Your Ears Hang Low?" shattered the neighborhood's peace. The kids on the playground scattered toward their houses, screaming, "The ice cream truck's coming!"

Of course there was an ice cream truck in this picture-perfect neighborhood.

Gus finished his duty and stared at the approaching vehicle. Might as well indulge. After all, I *was* on vacation.

The kelly green and white truck lumbered closer and stopped

a few houses down. I gathered a few bills from my purse and waited with Gus next to Laura's mailbox.

"I want ice creaaaam!" a child's voice screeched.

I whipped around. A red-faced boy in fire-engine print swim trunks dragged a man with a five o'clock shadow out of the blue house and into the yard.

"You already had a cookie." The man wore khaki pants and a Thurston's Marina T-shirt, and gray hairs fringed his temples.

The kid stomped his bare feet in the grass. "I want a bomb pop."

Heaving a sigh, the man withdrew a few bills from his pocket and handed them to the boy.

"Thank you, Daddy!" He darted across the street to the playground to join the other kids who were returning after bilking money out of their parents.

The man leaned against a gray minivan with a stick-figure family of three decal on the rear window. He didn't appear to notice Gus and me.

A door slammed. "Keith Thurston!" A tiny blond woman wearing gray scrubs thundered onto the porch. "Don't you dare tell me you're letting him have ice cream!"

Oh boy.

"Just a bomb pop." He didn't look at the woman but kept his gaze fixed on the playground.

"You always let him have his way." She threw her hands in the air. "I'm done. I'm literally *done!* I can't deal with this after working all day."

The man didn't flinch at this pronouncement, and I suspected he'd heard those words before.

"You think I'm kidding?"

Seconds ticked by, and the only sound was the ice cream truck's song, which had changed to "Pop Goes the Weasel." New lyrics came to mind, and I choked back a laugh, though nothing about this was funny.

All around the lake neighborhood, the wife's rant reached the neighbors. The husband stood and took it all in. Pop—!

She slugged his arm. "Answer me." She tacked on a few choice words that made me want to bend over and cover Gus's ears. I hoped the kids at the playground weren't listening.

"What's there to say, Rachel? I never get it right."

"Fine," she hissed. "As soon as Julian's in bed, I'm out of here, and you can raise him however you want. First thing Monday, I'm filing for divorce." She stomped into the house and slammed the door.

My heart ached as my gaze fell on the kids across the street. Poor Julian. His world was about to be rocked. I said a silent prayer for God to help this young family.

The ice cream truck, with a white, oval-shaped sign that read *Clover's Ice Cream,* edged closer and parked at the playground. The kids swarmed around pushing and shoving to be first in line.

As Gus and I crossed the street, the tin-panny music stopped. We hung back while a fresh-faced gal who couldn't have been more than twenty-five hopped out and took the kids' orders. She wore a white polo with a kelly green logo that matched the truck and denim cutoffs more like underwear than shorts. At least she was thin enough to pull it off. My legs would look like overstuffed sausages.

When the kids had scattered, I approached the truck.

"Smart," Miss Underwear Shorts said. "Waiting for the coast to clear." She glanced over my shoulder, and her golden-brown ponytail swung. "My ice cream doesn't usually cause parents to have knock-down-drag-outs. But you see a little bit of everything."

"I can imagine."

"Cute dog." She nodded at Gus. "Mind if I give him a biscuit?"

"Not at all."

She reached in her truck, procured the treat, and tossed it at Gus, who snapped it up in one bite. He wagged his tail.

She'd made a friend for life.

"What can I get you?"

I studied the menu. "Ice cream sandwich."

"Coming right up." She retrieved the sandwich. "I haven't seen you around. You new?"

"Visiting a friend." I held out my money. "Nice neighborhood."

"I make a killing around here with all these rich lake people who can't say no to their kids." She took my bills and made change.

Interesting that she felt free to make that comment to me without knowing my background. "Never stand between a kid and his ice cream." That should be Life Lesson #588.

"For reals." She dropped a few coins into my hand. "Just last weekend, this super rich guy over on Sunset Beach hired my truck for one of his teenage son's fancy-schmancy parties." She looked around and lowered her voice. "Those teenagers were ten times more immature than any five-year-old I've seen since I started this gig. They bought ice cream for a food fight." She grimaced. "I made a ton of money, but I hate waste, you know?"

"I get it. You own the truck?" I pocketed my change, twisted Gus's leash around my wrist, unwrapped my ice cream, and took a bite.

"Yep. I'm Clover." She pointed to the sign, and I noticed a tattoo of a small, four-leaf clover on her right wrist.

I swallowed. "I'm Georgia, and I grew up on a farm, so this is my first experience with an ice cream truck."

She arched a perfectly shaped eyebrow and gazed at me as if

she weren't sure if I was telling the truth. "Wow . . . that's . . . super sad. Happy to be of service." She hopped back in the truck and saluted. "See ya."

I took another bite of ice cream and watched the truck mosey around the neighborhood loop before turning onto the road that circled the lake.

"Yoo-hoo!"

I flinched and nearly choked on my ice cream. I turned toward the sound, and a pudgy woman in a Notre Dame T-shirt waved from the yellow cottage's front porch. She pressed a fluffy gray cat to her chest. I'd heard that sometimes people looked like their animals, and in this woman's case, that was true. Like her cat, she had wispy gray hair and scrunched up features.

Life Lesson #11,899: Always adopt a cute pet.

"Georgia?" she called.

"Yes, ma'am." Gus and I crossed the yard.

"Howdy! I'm Sheila Thurston, and this is Pickles." She looked at her pet and held out a key. "I thought you might need this. Beautiful dog."

Gus inched closer, and Pickles eyed him with disdain.

"Thanks." As I took the key, a bit of vanilla ice cream dripped onto my hand.

"Don't let me stop you from eating." Sheila's gaze lingered on my ice cream sandwich with an intensity that rivaled Gus's longing.

No worries. I licked the drop from my hand and took another bite.

"Enjoy it while you're young. Someday you'll be post-menopausal, and your metabolism will go AWOL." She tugged her T-shirt hem over her hips. "But you're tall, so your extra pounds have plenty of room to spread out."

Merciful heavens. This conversation had taken a wrong turn into Awkwardville.

"But you've got years before you have to worry about that," she said. "Laura tells me you're a farmer. How's a pretty girl like you get into a profession like that?"

Yikes. "My dad and grandpa farmed, and my brother wasn't interested."

"You married?"

"No, ma'am."

"Boyfriend?"

"Dating a great guy." I finished the last of my ice cream and crumpled the wrapper into a wad. *For now.* I pushed Hamlet Miller out of my mind.

"Good for you. My husband of thirty-seven years passed away two years ago. I'm finally feeling alive again. Pickles has helped. We rescued each other."

"I'm sorry for your loss."

"Thanks. It was his time because he was suffering from cancer, but that didn't make it any easier. Now, tell me how you know Laura. I tried to ask her, but she didn't have time to chat. She's one busy lady. I'm not sure how she makes time for that boyfriend of hers, but I'm not sure that's a bad thing." She pressed her fingers to her mouth. "There I go again. Giving my opinion where it's not needed or wanted. My son tells me all the time to stop, and it drives my daughter-in-love crazy, but I can't help myself. Do you ever have that trouble?"

I wanted to answer, but I wasn't sure which question to tackle first. It wasn't often that someone had me beat in the babbling department.

"I apologize," she continued. "I'll let you draw your own conclusions about Laura's beau, but I'd like to state for the record that she can do better. How *do* you know Laura?"

"We went to the same elementary school and have been friends ever since." That was the short version.

In truth, Laura Patterson moving to Wildcat Springs in the

middle of fifth grade had been an answer to my prayers after my former best friend Sarah Beckmann had decided being buddies with a gawky music nerd, whose other pastime included following her daddy around the farm, wasn't so cool. She'd dumped me for Gina Conyers, and they'd remained besties until Gina stole Sarah's boyfriend not long after high school.

"Isn't that sweet," Sheila said. "I hope you have a good visit, and don't let the drama next door bother you."

"Oh?" Listening was currently my friend, and I wasn't going to risk saying more than I should.

"You're a polite one, aren't you? Don't deny you heard Keith and Rachel's argument. I saw you watching." She petted her cat.

"I was waiting on the ice cream truck." Why, oh why, did I feel the need to offer an excuse to Mrs. McNosy?

"I didn't mean anything by that, but my daughter-in-love's screeches are hard to miss. If she follows through and leaves, my son and grandson will be better off."

Whoa. And yet she still called Rachel her *daughter-in-love*. Weird. In my head, I could hear my friend Brandi admonishing against gossip, and she'd be right on.

"Keith's been miserable ever since Rachel got pregnant, and he felt like he had to marry her. She was too young and wasn't ready to be tied down." Sheila flicked her gaze toward the house. "I say she's been having an affair. But listen to me. Chewing your ear off when you'd like to go in and relax." She looked past me and pointed. "There's Laura now."

She waved as Laura's black Camaro stopped in the driveway. "You girls have a nice visit." She and Pickles returned to the house.

"Georgia!" Laura squealed, clopped across the cement driveway in her pink high-heeled pumps, and held out her hands for a hug. "It's so good to see you. I have sooo much to tell you!"

Laura's house had a screened-in porch facing the channel in her backyard, and the opposite side of the waterway was tree lined, making for a peaceful view. She'd painted the porch walls and beams a creamy white and decorated the gray wicker furniture with cushions in a blue fish print. A ceiling fan whirred, stirring the humid air flowing in through the open windows.

After Laura changed out of her gray power suit into navy shorts and a sailboat-print tank top, we curled up on the opposite ends of the sofa facing the water. Gus snoozed next to the door that led to the patio. Apparently, the trip had exhausted him.

"What's your news?" Thanks to Sheila I had a pretty good idea what Laura was about to tell me, but I didn't want to let on.

Laura twisted her wavy black hair into a bun, secured it with a clip, and propped her feet on the coffee table. Her bright blue eyes were framed by dark lashes that I'd been envious of for years. My lashes were of the pale variety that needed globs of mascara to even think about showing up.

"I've met *the one*."

"That's wonderful." I didn't have any trouble looking surprised, considering this information carried a twist I hadn't been expecting. "I need details."

"His name's Tommy Ferraro. He's handsome, and he's a golf pro at Hideaway Country Club. We met last fall when I was visiting my parents, and he's part of the reason I moved here."

Even though Laura's well-to-do parents had moved to Lake Hideaway not long after we'd graduated high school, I'd been a little surprised she'd relocated. That was one mystery solved. "I'm glad to have you back in Indiana." I flicked my honey-blond braid back and forth between my fingers and considered the most important question of all. "Is Tommy a Christian?"

"Oh yes."

But she said it a little too quickly. Maybe I was imagining things since Sheila had already shared her thoughts about Laura's boyfriend. Why should the opinion of a gossipy neighbor matter when Laura seemed happy?

"I can't wait for you to meet him." She clasped her hands, reminding me of the kids who'd been waiting on the ice cream truck. "He's on his way now, and we're going for a sunset cruise around the lake."

"That sounds perfect."

I promised myself that I'd keep an open mind prior to meeting Tommy Ferraro, but we weren't even out of the channel and onto the lake before I was on Team Sheila regarding his suitability as a potential mate for my childhood buddy.

I had three reasons.

First, he looked me up and down upon his arrival, and his squirrelly eyes had lingered a little too long on my chest, in spite of the fact I was wearing a modest and rather boring green-striped T-shirt. He wasn't bad looking, though his slicked-back hair was receding, and he was a few inches shorter than me.

Second, he wore a thick gold chain around his neck, and that item of business shouldn't need further explanation.

Third, he'd winked and told Laura, "Baby doll, I'll drive the boat. I'd hate for you to be gabbing so much you don't watch where you're goin' and crash into somebody's pier."

My friend, who was an accomplished and fully capable attorney, gave him a kiss and told him how wonderful he was for looking out for her. It was at this point that I'd begun to wonder if I was dealing with Stepford Laura.

At the very least, my visit was going to be interesting.

Tommy eased the speedboat past the bobbing orange buoys

welcoming us onto the lake that spanned over three thousand acres. I scooted to the edge of my seat, trying to get my bearings and remember all the landmarks I'd learned through the years while visiting Grandma and Grandpa Smith. After he and Grandma had died, Mom and Aunt Janie had sold their cottage, and I hadn't been here since.

To the south, the small village of Hidden Shores was nestled along the lake's edge. Grandma and Grandpa's place had been on the outskirts of town. To the north, there was a large marsh, Smith Bay, Calloway Cove, and a winding channel that led to Little Hideaway, a tiny fishing lake with a few inhabitants and where motorboats were only allowed to idle.

Because we had some time before sunset, Tommy zoomed across the choppy water at full speed. Laura was sitting next to him but faced me in the back. She tried to tell me something, but when I couldn't hear her, she grinned and shook her head.

As water splashed my face, I spotted familiar majestic homes lining the lake's shore. White piers with flagpoles jutted into the water, and American flags waved. People also pledged their allegiance to their favorite colleges—and Purdue and IU flags dominated.

My mind strayed, and I wished Hamlet could be here with me. It'd be fun sharing my memories with him, but lately, he was wrapped up in his own ambitions, and I wasn't sure what that meant for us as a couple.

Refusing to dwell on him, I turned my attention to the boats squeezing in water time before sunset. We passed a pontoon towing two screeching kids on a tube, and a guy on a personal watercraft buzzed past, a rooster tail spraying a stream of water behind him.

Tommy slowed as we reached the middle of the lake that had an optimal view of the sunset. He cut the engine, and we floated, the water lapping against the hull. Since there weren't boats nearby, he didn't drop an anchor. He moved over to Laura's seat and snuggled with her. She gazed at him with adoring eyes.

I was being too judgmental and needed to give him a chance. If Laura thought he was wonderful, then I'd keep an open mind.

"What do you like most about being a golf pro?" I asked Tommy.

"I meet some fascinating people." He squared his shoulders. "I played with Byron Collins and the governor of Michigan today."

Laura turned to me. "Byron Collins is the mayor of Hidden Shores." She swatted Tommy playfully. "I've heard Governor Milton is thinking about running for president. That's exciting, Tom-Tom. Hobnobbing with power players."

Tom-Tom? Someone send a barf bag.

"Governor Milton's parents have a place on Hideaway, so he plays our course when he's visiting," he said. "Byron invited me to join them. I gave Darwin a few free tips about his swing and—"

"So you're on a first-name basis with the governor?" Laura gushed.

Tommy winked. "Yep. *Darwin* had one of his most awesome rounds ever." He sounded proud of himself, which was clearly his standard operating procedure.

"Good for him." I didn't love politics—or golf.

"You play, Georgia?" Tommy asked.

"No." Chasing a ball around a green pasture was dumb, but I couldn't insult this man's life work no matter how smarmy I thought he was. "I'm not athletically inclined. Just ask Laura."

"Unless I was team captain, she was always picked last in PE."

Thanks for dredging up that little factoid.

"True story." I fixed my gaze on the horizon, where the sun cast glistening orange light over the lake. Wispy clouds fluttering above the tree line took on a pink hue.

"Tell you what," Tommy said. "If you and Laura wanna hit balls at the driving range sometime this week, I'd be happy to give you some pointers."

I pictured him trying to cop a feel while adjusting my swing. *No. Thank you.* "We'll see if it fits into our schedule." I hoped Laura would take my polite hint, but the way she'd turned all googly eyed over her boyfriend, I couldn't be sure my extremely intelligent friend was functioning at full capacity.

Why did Hamlet have to be wrapped up in rehearsals? I could've used a protective detail right about now, and one icy look from my boyfriend would settle Tommy. Hamlet might be lanky, but he was tough.

"Georgia water skis," Laura said. "So she does do *something* athletic."

"There's an amateur water-skiing competition later this week. You gonna participate?" Tommy smirked as if he already knew the answer.

"You never know. I might surprise you." Who was I kidding? It'd been years since I'd skied.

"How about I come over early tomorrow morning, and we take the boat out before it gets busy?" he asked. "You can brush up."

There was no mistaking the challenge in his voice.

Laura pressed her hand to his chest. "Baby, that'd be awesome." She turned to me. "The water's like glass at six thirty."

"Six-thirty?" My eyes bugged. I wasn't a stranger to early morning farm work, but this was supposed to be my vacation. My family had never gotten up early to ski, and sometimes it took us until early afternoon to even make it out on the boat.

"You can take a nap to catch up on your beauty sleep later." Tommy winked.

I was trying to like Tommy, but he was making it so . . . *diffi-*

cult. I produced a fake smile. "I guess we'll see you bright and early."

"Perfect. I'll bring coffee and donuts," he said.

It'd take a gallon of coffee to offset a dose of Tommy Ferraro at the crack of dawn.

After sunset, we returned to Laura's house, and Tommy stuck around until almost midnight droning on and on about all the supposedly famous people who played golf at Hideaway Country Club. After he left, Laura and I had been too tired to engage in serious gabbing, so I made my way upstairs to the spacious guest bedroom with an attached bathroom.

The room was painted a pale blue and overlooked the channel in the backyard. A rustic, metal headboard framed the queen bed, and flowered pillows accented a crisp white comforter.

A perfect place to relax and forget my troubles.

While I tossed the pillows on a gray armchair in the corner, I thought back to the sunny afternoon a couple of weeks earlier when Hamlet had called and told me he'd wanted to come over because he had exciting news.

While Gus snoozed in his crate, I'd made lemonade from powder—because this girl didn't keep lemons on hand. I was carrying the glasses onto the back porch of my farmhouse when Hamlet arrived.

His handsome, chiseled face displayed a broad grin, and his lanky frame was taller than mine—which I appreciated because I towered over a lot of men.

I put the glasses on the table beside the wicker loveseat. "I had a domestic moment and made lemonade."

"That sounds refreshing." He drew me into his arms and gave

me a quick peck on the lips. "I had the most wonderful thing happen today." He squeezed my hand.

"What's that?"

"I was cast as Professor Harold Hill in *The Music Man* at Bell's Dinner Theater." His blue-gray eyes shone.

I blinked. "Congratulations! You're perfect for the part." I threw my arms around him, and he picked me up and spun me around. "Why didn't you tell me you auditioned?" He'd spent four years after college acting in theater productions all over the country and had recently returned to Wildcat Springs to focus on flipping houses.

"I didn't tell anyone," he said. "I wanted it to be a surprise."

He'd succeeded.

"Lately I've been thinking how much I've missed acting, so I decided to audition. It feels wonderful to know I'll be on stage again."

"When does the show open?" I asked.

"August, so I'll be very busy these next few weeks."

"Let's sit. I want to know all about it."

"I'm sorry. I can't stay because I need to get to our first rehearsal." He drained the lemonade in a few gulps and set the sweaty glass back on the table.

"Okay." This whirlwind visit was making my head spin as I tried not to worry about what this new development could mean for our future.

"Thanks for the lemonade." He kissed me and then headed for his truck. "I'll call you tonight."

As I watched him drive away, I tried to figure out what'd happened to the attentive man I'd been dating. His absentmindedness had gotten worse as time passed, and he became even busier, juggling his rehearsals and construction work.

When Laura had invited me to her new house, I'd jumped at the chance. My best friend Brandi was visiting World War II historical sites in Europe because of a teacher appreciation grant that she'd won. My other best friend Ashley had traveled to Michigan for a family reunion with her boyfriend—my cousin J.T.

I plopped onto the bed hoping the new scenery and time with an old buddy would give me a new perspective—if Tommy butted out long enough for Laura and me to have some peace.

CHAPTER TWO

E ven though I hadn't acquired a coffee-guzzling habit until
college, Laura knew about my caffeine addiction. When I
stumbled out of her guest bedroom the next morning, two travel
mugs waited in the kitchen, filled with the coffee Tommy had
brought. Gus wasn't a morning dog, and when I put on his life
vest, he didn't even fight me.

I snagged some towels, picked up my mug, and led Gus
outside. When I shuffled across the dewy grass, my feet slipped
back and forth over my flip-flops. Even though it was early, the
humidity hung in the fishy-smelling air. Gus bounded ahead to
the boat where Tommy was loading in the life jackets, skis, a
kneeboard, and a wakeboard.

"Hey, boy!" Tommy scratched Gus's head.

Gus sat beside the boat and looked back at me as if he weren't
sure how to proceed. Or he wasn't a fan of Tommy. I helped the
dog on board, and I took my spot in the stern while Gus sniffed
the bow.

A bare-chested Tommy eyed my shorts and T-shirt. "You

wearin' a swimsuit under all that?" He straightened his shoulders as if he wanted me to admire his hairy pecs. And, yes, he was still wearing the gold chain.

"Yep." I lifted the edge of my shirt, so he could see a teeny-tiny sliver of my red one piece. I didn't own a bikini, but if I did, it would've stayed safely tucked in my suitcase as long as Tommy was around.

"Tommy brought donuts." Laura, clad in a yellow crocheted bikini and looking like she'd never ever ingested any sort of fried pastry, trotted toward the boat. She swung a white sack and carried a travel mug in her other hand.

"Thanks." I spread my towel on the seat and sat back down.

"Hidden Shores has the best donut shop in the Midwest, and the owner hooked me up. He's one of my pals."

Only the best for Tommy Ferraro.

Laura sat beside me as Tommy started the boat. "You have to try these. Tommy got the Breakfast Mayhem, and they have candied bacon on top." She plunged a napkin into the sack, removed a donut, and thrust it toward me as we idled down the channel.

I took the diet buster and popped a piece in my mouth as Gus wandered over, hoping I'd share. I tossed a tiny bacon piece in Gus's direction, and he downed it in a single snap.

"They *are* good." The bacon was a nice contrast to the sweet caramel icing. I sipped the coffee. One point for Tommy. Winstons were fair, and I had to credit him with providing a tasty breakfast.

No one else in the neighborhood was stirring except the birds in the trees flanking the channel, and as we approached the lake, placid water beckoned. I'd never seen Lake Hideaway so calm. Normally the heavy boat traffic caused waves that bounced off the seawalls, compounding the water's roughness.

"Perfect skiing water," Tommy said. "Ain't it worth getting up early?"

I'd learned to ski on rough water, so it didn't matter one way or the other to me. "It's cool seeing the lake so calm." *Nice Georgia.* That was diplomatic, wasn't it?

While I finished my donut, Tommy hit full speed and navigated into Smith Bay. This area of the lake was smoother than the main body of water because the bay was partially surrounded by a marsh and a beach that allowed the waves to dissipate.

On the shore opposite the marsh was a narrow peninsula that held Lakeview Park. The small public area had a sandy beach, piers, a boat ramp, and picnic benches. The walking and biking trail that circled the lake blazed a path through the park. Even so, the entire area was nearly deserted, with only a single car in the lot.

On the other side of the peninsula was the secluded Calloway Cove that wasn't quite big enough for skiing or tubing but was a fun place to take a WaveRunner and do some 360s.

Tommy stopped the boat in the middle of Smith Bay, and we were the only watercraft around. "You're up, Georgia. Ladies— and guests—first."

I took a swig of coffee and gazed at the marsh, where the sea of cattails swayed in the breeze. "How's the water temperature?"

"Last I checked, it's eighty-five degrees or so." Tommy attached the rope to the boat and tossed it into the water. "Nice and comfy."

I buckled on my life vest, swung my legs onto the wood platform, and let the water wash over my toes. It was warmer than the current air temperature, so I jumped in without a shriek. I swiped water out of my face and tossed a clump of slimy weeds that tickled my arm.

Tommy slipped the skis into the water. "Keep your knees bent, and let the boat pull you up."

"Tom-Tom, she remembers," Laura said.

I sure did. I gritted my teeth as I slipped on the skis.

"I'm sorry. It's just the teacher in me." He winked.

I'd never been a fan of the term *mansplaining*, but now, after meeting Tommy, I understood why some women used the word. I caught the rope and gave him a thumbs up. "Ready."

Tommy eased the boat forward until the rope was taut and then gunned the engine. I shot out of the water with a teeny burst of pride that I'd only needed one try. If I'd truly wanted to show off, I should've tried to slalom.

As I flew through the air, goosebumps rose on my arms and legs. Dropping back into the warm water would feel good, but I definitely wasn't ready to quit any time soon.

Tommy followed the shoreline past the beach and turned back toward the marsh. I moved my skis to the right and buzzed over the wake onto the silky water reflecting the morning sun. For a few seconds, I felt as if I were racing the boat, and I reached out and batted a cylindrical white buoy.

Laura cheered, and Gus wiggled next to her.

As we passed the cattails, I shifted and zipped back toward the wake, but at the last second, I hesitated and didn't hit it straight on. The edge of my left ski caught the wake, and I lost my balance.

Throwing the rope away, I slammed against the water, my shoulder absorbing the blow. My skis rocketed off as the water swallowed me. I resurfaced sputtering and groaning.

This was what happened when I tried to show off.

I blinked water from my eyes and tried to catch my breath. At least I didn't have to worry about boat traffic, but out of habit, I glanced around. My skis were floating away, so I swam after them.

As I moved forward, weeds brushed against the back of my

leg. I flinched, but then something solid bumped into the back of my arm.

A snake from the marsh? I shuddered as I whipped around. No. Much worse than a snake. A scream built in my throat.

A human body floated facedown next to me.

CHAPTER THREE

A hybrid scream-gasp escaped my lips. My heart thudded, and I flailed my limbs in a clumsy attempt to put distance between the corpse and me. Tommy and Laura whirred along while she fed him donut bits, lovebirds completely oblivious to the fact I'd fallen into a scene from a horror movie.

Seriously? "Come on, Gus. Help me out here. Bark!" I shouted.

When I reached one of my skis, I seized it and held it straight out in front of me. Not that I wanted to disrespect the body of a person made in God's image, but if I had to gently tap the corpse with my ski to keep it at bay, I would.

While I took a steadying breath, I surveyed the poor soul. It was a man with short blond hair and broad shoulders. He wore running shorts, and a gray T-shirt with white trim around the neck and sleeves. My eyes fell on the single car in the park's lot. Had the victim been swimming at the public beach and drowned? No. He was wearing athletic shoes. Maybe someone had hit him with a car while he was running and then dumped his body.

My throat ached. Whatever the circumstance, this man's family would be facing one of the worst days of their lives.

Comfort them, Lord.

Tommy and Laura finally noticed I'd fallen, and the boat turned toward me. When they were a couple hundred yards away, Tommy slowed. Laura leaned over and fished out the other ski before they idled closer. Gus rushed to the bow, looked out at me, and barked. If Laura hadn't grabbed his collar, he would've jumped overboard.

"There's a man's body." My voice trembled as I pointed to my right. If I hadn't already been through the experience of finding someone dead, this occurrence would've been ten times harder.

Tommy cut the engine and looked at me as if I'd lost my mind. "What'd you say, sweetheart?"

"A corpse bumped into me." I pointed a drippy finger again.

He rushed to the port side and peered over. Laura gasped and covered her mouth with her hand. Tommy's eyes grew huge, and he stood frozen while Laura, still holding onto Gus, fumbled in her beach bag before removing her phone.

It finally occurred to me that I should get out of the water, so I kicked my way to the boat and hauled myself onto the platform while Laura called 9-1-1.

"Georgia Winston. I'm sorry we're meeting again under these circumstances." Detective Ryan McCloud with the Webster County Sheriff's Department held out his hand. "But it's nice to see you."

We shook hands. "Likewise." I guessed he was about forty-five judging by the gray streaks in his dark brown hair and the lines around his kind, gray eyes.

He stooped and patted Gus's head. We were standing on the

sandy shore of Lakeview Park where we'd docked after the deputies and recovery team had arrived and relieved us of body protection duties. Since it was still early, only a few walkers and joggers passed by on the trail. Most of them slowed to take in the commotion.

"How do you know Detective McCloud?" Laura's forehead creased as she and Tommy exchanged glances.

"Long story." I clutched Gus's leash tighter and ground my flip flop into the sand. "I'll tell you later."

"Do we have an ID for the victim?" Laura cinched her cover-up tie.

Detective McCloud flicked his gaze toward Tommy and me before turning toward Laura. "Not yet. He wasn't carrying ID. The one vehicle in the lot belongs to a guy who just finished his morning jog, so the victim didn't park here." He clamped his mouth shut.

She nodded. They'd clearly discuss more details when Tommy and I weren't around. Her new position as a deputy prosecutor in Webster County certainly made it easy for her to get information. If I'd asked these questions at home, I'd have been shut down.

As the team had removed the man's body from the water, I'd tried to catch a glimpse of his face, but we'd been too far away. Still, I figured we'd learn his identity soon enough.

"Did he drown, or did someone whack him?" Tommy asked. "'Cause people don't go for a swim in running shoes."

Merciful heavens. I sneaked a peek at my friend, but she didn't flinch. How had she ever gotten used to this man?

"We won't know until the autopsy results are released." Detective McCloud swept his gaze over Tommy, who still hadn't bothered to don a shirt. "How about I get your statements, and the three of you can go enjoy the rest of your day—or at least try to."

Laura rested her hand on Tommy's forearm. "We'd appreciate that."

"Yes. Thank you." I stifled a sigh. So much for getting more information. But if I were Detective McCloud, I'd want to get rid of us too.

Once Laura, Tommy, and I had given our statements, we'd decided we needed a more substantial breakfast than donuts. After we dropped Gus off at Laura's house and changed clothes, Tommy drove us across the lake to Lachlan's Lighthouse.

This restaurant on Sunrise Point was housed in a white stucco building attached to a small red and white striped lighthouse that existed for show. However, as a kid I'd thought it was cool to climb to the top and peer through the glass at the lake. At that time, the restaurant had been known as The Lighthouse, so I figured the place had changed hands and hoped the food was still good. A whiff of spicy sausage gave me hope.

Tommy docked the boat at a pier near the main building, and since all the tables inside were full, we found an empty one on the weathered wooden deck surrounding the lighthouse. We gazed out at the choppy water crashing into the seawall while we waited for a server to take our orders. A steady breeze kept the rising temperature bearable, and a couple of gulls cawed as they flew overhead.

"How could you be so calm this morning?" Tommy stood and adjusted the umbrella above our table to provide more shade.

"I didn't feel calm, but this wasn't my first rodeo." I smoothed my damp hair and fixed my gaze on the sailboats racing across the lake. "I found a body in the woods next to my field last year during harvest."

"Whoa. That's freaky." He'd finally put on a polo shirt, to the relief of everyone who wasn't a fan of hairy chests.

"It was." I shuddered at the memory. No one deserved to end up that way.

"Georgia's even helped her local sheriff's department solve some other cases." Laura sipped her water.

"You gonna help find who killed the poor guy?" Tommy rested his elbows on the table. "I ain't buying that he accidentally drowned."

I unrolled my silverware. "I'm sure Detective McCloud and his department can handle the job."

"Absolutely. Ryan is an excellent detective." Laura tipped her sunglasses and peered at her boyfriend.

"All right. I can take a hint." His phone was ringing, so he got up. "Excuse me. I gotta take this. If our waitress comes, order me a meat lover's omelet." He sauntered toward the deck's railing and stood facing the water.

A waitress finally stopped at our table, and I stifled a gasp when I took in her gray T-shirt with white trim.

Just like the victim's.

"I apologize for the wait," she said. "I'm Alexa, and I'll be taking care of you."

I put her age at about thirty, and she had dark eyebrows and short, platinum hair. "No problem," I said. "We can see you're swamped."

"One of our guys didn't show for work." She huffed. "Of all the mornings for Aaron to bail, but he's never been reliable for morning shifts," she muttered.

Could Aaron be the man I'd found, or had he simply overslept?

"What can I get you?" Alexa stood poised with her pen against a notepad.

I shifted my focus back to our server, and Laura and I ordered omelets.

"Would you like more biscuits and muffins?" she asked.

Before I could decline, Laura held out the empty basket. "Absolutely."

Having a metabolism that moved at the speed of Indy cars had to be nice.

Alexa took the container and hurried away, and I turned to Laura. "Did you notice her shirt matched the victim's?"

"Yes." Laura glanced around. "All the servers have gray shirts with white trim."

"What if Aaron didn't come to work because he's the man in the water?" I whispered.

Laura picked up her phone, and her fingers flew across the device. "I'm checking to see if Ryan will send me the victim's name as soon as he knows."

In other words, she didn't want me asking our server more questions. I'd respect that. Instead, I fished my phone from my straw tote, found the restaurant's social media page, and scrolled through pictures of the servers in action. It didn't take long to find one with a broad-shouldered, blond server and bartender named Aaron who wore a wedding band and couldn't have been more than thirty. The caption didn't give his last name or tag him in the post.

Tommy strolled toward us. "Your boyfriend texting you?"

Before I could put my phone away, he peeked over my shoulder.

"I know him!" Tommy pushed his sunglasses up on his head and whipped around. "Why're you—?"

I tracked his squinty gaze across the patio to where Alexa was refilling coffee mugs at an elderly couple's table.

"Her shirt looks like. . ." He turned back toward us. "Are you two thinkin' the guy in the picture could be the float—?"

"Shhh!" Laura squeezed his forearm. "We don't want anything getting out before the sheriff's department is ready to release information to the public," she whispered.

He sat. "Gotcha." He lowered his voice to a whisper and pointed toward my phone. "I talked to that guy, Aaron Lehman, when he was bartending. Nice dude." He motioned toward the tiki bar in the corner. "Married to my ex-girlfriend's sister, but Nora and I were through before he came into the picture. Father-in-law owns Sutcliffe Marina." He shook his head. "What a shame," he mumbled.

I shoved my phone in my purse as Alexa approached with more biscuits and muffins. Just what my thighs needed. Extra carbs. But the muffins were made with fresh blueberries. And I *was* on vacation.

How many times could a girl legitimately use that excuse?

"It'll be a while yet on the rest of your food." Alexa set the basket on the table. "I'm sorry." She topped off our sweaty water glasses and hustled away.

"Excuse me. I'm going to hit the restroom." I took my bag from the back of the chair and threaded through the patio tables. When I entered the restaurant, the air conditioning chilled me. Dropping my sunglasses into my tote, I followed boat-shaped signs down a paneled back hall to the restroom. Clatters and shouts sounded in the kitchen as I pushed into the ladies' room.

After I took care of business, a woman's bellowing voice caused me to freeze with my paper towel covered hand on the restroom door.

"What do you mean you don't know where my husband is?"

I cracked the door and peered out. Alexa cowered against the wall as a red-haired, pregnant woman in a black maxi dress encroached on Alexa's personal space.

Whoa.

Alexa held up both hands. "I swear. I don't know where

Aaron is. If I did, I'd tell you, because I'm ticked that he didn't show this morning."

If Pregnant Lady was asking about her husband Aaron, then she was Tommy's ex-girlfriend's sister. What had he said their last name was?

Lehman.

Mrs. Lehman slapped Alexa. "You've been having an affair with him, you bleach blonde tramp!" She pointed to her large belly. "How could you do this to us when we're having a baby?" Her freckly complexion reddened.

"I didn't." Alexa covered her face with her hands and shrank against the paneling. "It's not me," she wailed. "Aaron and I are just friends!"

Mrs. Lehman closed her eyes and clenched her fists as if she were trying to subdue her rage. Her eyes flew open. "I don't believe you!"

Alexa flinched, and even I jumped.

Where was the manager or the other employees? Should I be ready to jump in and yank this woman off of Alexa? Clearly, she didn't want to fight an expectant mother, even though she was on the verge of being beaten to a pulp. Not to mention, Mrs. Lehman's toned arms advertised that she spent a lot of time in the gym.

"Okay, okay. Aaron and I aren't together, but I do know who he's seeing." Alexa spread her fingers apart and peeked between them.

Mrs. Lehman took a menacing step forward. "Who?"

"Some nurse named Rachel."

CHAPTER FOUR

Could Alexa be talking about Laura's neighbor Rachel Thurston? Sheila's daughter-in-love who'd scolded her husband loud enough for the entire subdivision to hear? Rachel had been wearing scrubs, which meant she might be a nurse. Plus, Sheila suspected Rachel was having an affair.

"You're lying." Mrs. Lehman's face twisted as she lunged at the poor waitress. "Rachel's his cousin. Tell me who he's been seeing!"

Okay, then. Not Rachel.

Alexa whimpered and pressed her back to the wall. "If it's not Rachel, then I swear I don't know. She's the only woman I've ever seen him with!"

"But you've heard somethi—"

"Dee, you need to settle down, or I'm calling the police," a middle-aged, burly man in a Cubs cap said as he exited the kitchen. "I can't have you treating my employees like this." He crossed hairy arms.

Dee Lehman whirled around and faced the man, giving

Alexa a chance to dart into the safety of the kitchen. "Do you know who my husband is seeing?" She sniffled.

"I don't." He unearthed a hanky from his pocket, shook it, and handed it to Dee. "I don't even know for a fact if Aaron is having an affair or why he didn't come in this morning."

She rested her hand on her belly. "You're only saying that because I'm pregnant."

"No, ma'am." He lifted his cap off his head and put it on backwards. "I don't have any idea."

"Do you know where he is?" She swiped her cheeks. "I haven't heard from him since Thursday evening."

The man looked at his sneakers. Had he heard about the man in the water and come to the same conclusion we had? Or did he know *why* the victim was in the water in the first place? Maybe he even knew about the affair and didn't want to admit it.

"I don't. I'm sorry," he said gently. "Have you filed a missing person report?"

"You think I should?"

"Yes." He cleared his throat. "I'll go with you to the sheriff's department if you want."

"Thank you, Lachlan." Dee's chin trembled.

"You're welcome." He reached toward her belly, but she caught his wrist.

He flinched.

"Seriously?" She scowled. "I'm not a petting zoo animal. Keep your hands to yourself." She let go of his wrist and muttered something that I probably didn't want to hear anyway.

"My apologies," he mumbled as he ducked his head and motioned for her to head down the narrow hallway first.

I stayed in the restroom until they passed. If Aaron had been having an affair, then his death might not be accidental.

Because of Tommy's presence, I kept what I'd learned in the restroom to myself when I returned to the table. I wasn't convinced I could trust him to be discreet, especially since he knew Dee Lehman.

Another server arrived with our food and told us Alexa had gone on break, so he'd be taking care of us for the rest of the time.

We devoured our omelets, and when Tommy took us back to Laura's house, I did a mental happy dance after he told us he had plans to play golf that afternoon with one of his buddies. Before I could slip into the house and give them privacy, he'd given Laura an uncomfortably long goodbye kiss right there in the backyard.

"What do you want to do now?" Laura asked as she entered her kitchen. "I *am* capable of driving my own boat, in spite of what Tommy says."

I gave Gus some fresh water, and he slurped it up. "Doesn't it bother you when Tommy makes comments like that?"

"He doesn't mean anything by it. He's a good guy." Her voice took on the slightest defensive edge.

I still needed convincing. "Let's chill on your porch and let our food settle." For some reason, I'd decided to consume most of the ginormous Western omelet and was still feeling the aftereffects of that poor decision. Laura opened the windows and turned on the ceiling fan, and we flopped on each end of the couch. Gus sprawled on his back, feet in the air.

"You never told me how you know Ryan McCloud," she said.

At least she'd waited to ask until Tommy had vamoosed. "Last spring, I was involved in a situation that brought me to Webster County, and he was the detective working the case." I gave her some more details about the adventure my stepsister Makayla and I had endured. At the time, Laura had been working for a high-powered law firm in Chicago.

"Wow. That's crazy. I'm glad everything turned out okay. I've heard about that case but had no idea you were involved." Laura dragged a pillow into her lap. "Whatever happened to the detective you were dating?"

My heart still twisted at the thought of Detective Cal Perkins. "I loved him, but he didn't feel the same. When I tried to get him to open up, he told me his life wasn't a mystery to solve. I didn't feel at peace about staying with a guy like that."

She grimaced. "Ouch. I'm sorry."

"Now we're friends. And neighbors—he bought Beverly Alspaugh's old place."

"Is that weird?"

"It's fine. I haven't seen him all that much lately." I waved once in a while when he was working in his yard or out running. After he'd encouraged me to date Hamlet, he'd kept his distance. Not being around Cal had helped me move on.

"What's the deal with you and Hamlet Miller? Is he as nerdy as he was in high school?"

I lifted my chin. "He's quirky—but very sweet. We've been exclusive for several months."

"Does he still wear sweater vests?" She smirked.

"Not in the summer, but yes."

"That's unfortunate."

I bristled. *Life Lesson #70,965: Women whose boyfriends wear obnoxious gold chains should not throw stones at sweater-vest wearers.* "It's just his thing. He wears flannel or T-shirts when he's renovating houses."

She snorted. "Like that's a vast improvement."

What was he supposed to wear? "He has a tattoo."

"Ooooh . . . his cool factor went up a few notches. G, I'm sorry. I know he's a good guy, but I have trouble picturing you with him long term. He's always been flaky. I feel like he's going to reel you in and then bail on you."

"You don't know that!" I picked a hangnail until it bled, which was a better option than punching Laura in the throat.

"Yeah, I do. His ex-girlfriend Carrie is one of my sister's best friends from college. Hamlet and Carrie were getting serious about marrying and moving to New York City when he decided big city life wasn't for him, and he wanted to go home to Wildcat Springs."

"So Hamlet prefers hamlets." I shrugged. "She could've followed him."

"She'd just gotten a role in a Broadway show."

"Well, maybe their relationship wasn't right. We don't know. And who are you to judge?"

She crossed her arms. "What's *that* supposed to mean?"

"You're dating a guy who treats you like you're helpless without his macho assistance. Is that really what you want?"

She shot up and tossed the throw pillow aside. "I *so* do not have to take this." She stomped inside and slammed the porch door so hard her cross-shaped suncatcher plopped onto the rug.

Gus hopped to his feet and sniffed it.

I stared out at the channel's smooth water and tried to absorb how quickly our conversation had deteriorated. *Should Gus and I head home?* I stood and hung the suncatcher that'd somehow stayed in one piece.

"I'm glad somebody's telling her the truth about that boyfriend of hers." With Pickles in her arms, Sheila hovered next to her porch's open window, and because the houses were so close, I had no doubt she'd listened to every word.

Privacy was one big reason I was glad I lived in the country. "Hi, Sheila." I tried not to sound annoyed, but it was a C+ effort —at best. I moved to Laura's window.

Gus put his paws on the ledge and wagged his tail at Pickles, who flicked her tail in response.

"Don't get in a hurry and leave," Sheila said. "Laura's sister visited a couple of weeks ago, and she made the exact observations you did. Laura reacted the same way. She got over it, and they had a nice time, so don't you worry." She stroked the cat. "All this heat makes people more aggressive. We need to get a nice, soaking rain to cool everything—and everybody—off."

"Did something else happen that makes you say that?" I had a bad habit of fishing for information. If I could ask enough subtle questions, Sheila might offer information without further coaxing.

"No. I was referring to Rachel and Keith's tiff last night. Not to mention, Rachel left late last night and didn't tell Keith where she was going."

"Maybe she went out with friends. Did you ever see her with another man?"

"Not exactly," she said. "But women don't leave their husbands unless they have another man waiting in the wings."

I wasn't so sure about that.

The porch door opened, and Laura stepped out. "G, can I talk to you a minute?"

"Sure. Nice to see you again, Sheila." Gus and I slipped into the kitchen, and I closed the door behind us.

"I'm sorry," Laura and I said in unison and laughed.

"How about we agree not to talk about men," I said. "And I'll keep an open mind about Tommy."

"Deal. I'll do the same with Hamlet." She leaned against the peninsula and held up her phone. "When I came in, I had a text from Detective McCloud about the victim's ID."

"And?"

"We were right. It's the bartender from Lachlan's Lighthouse, Aaron Lehman."

CHAPTER FIVE

"Aaron Lehman's wife Dee thinks he was having an affair," I said.

"What? You've been here less than twenty-four hours." Laura put her hands on her skinny hips, and her blue eyes widened. "How on earth could you *possibly* know that?"

I told her about Aaron's wife Dee accosting our waitress and how the restaurant's owner, Lachlan, seemed to leave the door open to the possibility of an affair. I explained how, because of Sheila, I'd suspected Rachel Thurston for about ten seconds before learning she and Aaron were cousins.

"Okay," she said. "That's seriously impressive. Leave it to you to overhear a conversation like that in the restroom."

"It does take a special talent—and a little luck." I grinned. "Now what?"

"Oh, no you don't. It's the weekend, and I'm off the crime-fighting clock. Plus, it's your vacation." She swiped her beach bag from the counter. "We're going swimming."

"While we wait on autopsy results?"

"No." She slipped her sunglasses onto her head. "To work on our tans."

Laura's subdivision had a designated beach for homeowners and their guests, so we loaded her childhood red wagon with pool noodles, rafts, and a cooler of water bottles and made our way to the shore. Picnic tables dotted a large grassy space, and sand covered a large patch directly behind the seawall. Puddles formed where water leaped over the breakwater, and plastic trucks, shovels, and buckets rested in the sand. A pier stretched into the lake.

Laura's neighbor Keith and his son Julian were the only ones in the water, and they tossed an orange frisbee back and forth. Julian squealed as the waves rocked up to his chin.

"Don't even think about it," Laura muttered as we placed the wagon in the shade of a silver maple next to a worn picnic table.

I removed my beach towel from my waist and squirted a glob of sunblock into my hand. "Give me some credit. His kid's here." I spread the coconut-scented lotion over my pasty legs that burned far too easily.

"Just checking."

"Have you talked to him much?" I whispered, though I didn't need to with the waves and boat motors.

"I moved in three months ago, and I've had an actual conversation with Keith and his wife maybe twice," she whispered. "We mostly wave and say *hello*. He's friendlier than she is."

"Did you ever hear them fight?"

She looked over her sunglasses. "The whole neighborhood has. It's practically a daily occurrence."

"Daddy, I want to play in the sand now." Julian flung the frisbee.

"Okay, buddy." He jumped and caught the disc that nearly flew above his reach.

They emerged from the water, and Keith dried his son off before Julian plopped down and loaded a dump truck with sand. Within seconds, his arms and legs were sand-coated.

Keith moseyed over to the cooler sitting on the picnic table. "He never wants to play in the sand *before* we swim." He unzipped the cooler and withdrew a beer bottle. "You ladies want one?"

"No thanks," I said.

"Laura?"

"No, I'm good. Thanks." She picked up a raft and headed for the water. I supposed she hoped I'd take the hint and follow, but I wasn't ready to walk away when Keith was in a semi-friendly mood. In the distance, sirens wailed, but unlike this morning, it was for a happier reason. The annual flotilla parade was beginning, and the decorated boats would soon pass the beach as they circled the lake.

I introduced myself to Keith while he used the edge of the picnic table to pop off the cap. "You live around here?" he asked.

"No. Wildcat Springs—near Richardville."

He took a swig of beer. "I went to college with a landscaper down there—Curtis Remington. His parents have a place here on Hideaway—Sunset Beach neighborhood. You know him?"

"Not well, but we've met through his wife Vanessa." Vanessa Hawk Remington was a detective with the Richard County Sheriff's Department and worked with my ex-boyfriend.

"They just got married, didn't they?"

"In April." I'd planned to attend the wedding with Cal—until we'd broken up.

Keith sat on the picnic table and rested his feet on the bench. "Hope they're happier than I've been." His face twisted with regret. "I'm sorry you had to witness that fight my wife and I had last evening. That's not how we like to welcome people to our neighborhood."

"Things happen."

He took a drink of beer and stared at the water. "Sure do. Don't let me keep you if you want to join Laura. I'm not good company." He rested his bottle on the table.

I slipped off my coverup. "I'll pray things get better for your family."

"I appreciate it." He didn't tear his gaze away from the lake.

I grabbed my raft, but before I could head to the water, Sheila buzzed up in a golf cart, and the distress on her face was obvious.

"Hey, Mom." Keith hopped off the table and approached her. "What's wrong?"

"I got a call on the prayer chain, and I'm afraid I have some bad news." She got out of the cart. "Aaron Lehman passed away."

"What!" Keith guided his mother to the picnic table. "Was there an accident?"

"They don't know for sure yet. Dee hadn't heard from him for a couple of days, and when she filed a missing-person report, she found out they"—her breath hitched—"they pulled his body out of the lake this morning. I had a terrible feeling when I heard the sirens, but I never would've guessed . . ."

I took a few steps toward the water, wondering how to gracefully step away without appearing insensitive.

Keith closed his eyes as the color drained from his face, and he leaned on the picnic table for support. "I need to find Rachel. She'll be devastated. Will you stay and watch Julian? He wants to see the flotilla."

"Of course." She glanced at her grandson.

As if he sensed her gaze, Julian looked up, threw aside his shovel, and ran over. "Grandma!"

"Hey, sweetheart." She opened her arms, and the sandy little boy hugged her ample waist.

I turned toward the water and slipped my raft in. When I glanced back toward the shore, Keith was driving away in his mother's golf cart, and Julian had returned to the sand and was watching the sheriff's department boat leading the parade as it passed. A pontoon decorated with a luau theme followed, and a woman in a grass skirt waved.

Sheila walked onto the pier. "Absolutely heartbreaking." She kicked off her silver flip flops and sat with her feet dangling in the water.

Towing the raft, I waded toward Sheila while Laura floated further from shore. "It is. Were Keith and Aaron close?" I lay face down on the raft and propped myself on my elbows.

"No, but Rachel thought the world of Aaron. They're cousins. His mother Emily and I were friends for ages until she died a couple of years ago. Keith's ten years older than Aaron, so they didn't really get to know each other until after Keith married Rachel."

"What was Aaron like?" If I could learn more about him, it'd take the edge off the memory of seeing his body floating next to me. A wave knocked me into the pier, and before it rocked me backward, I clutched the pier's metal post.

She brushed sand from the wooden slats. "According to my daughter-in-love, he's a solid guy—*now*. Served time for drug possession a while back. Before that, my husband gave Aaron a job working for our marina, but Aaron kept blowing off work. Ian finally fired him to keep peace with the other employees, and Aaron resented it for a long time. The last few years, he's been a bartender and server at Lachlan's Lighthouse. Got married to a nice gal named Dee, and they're expecting their first child—a miracle baby since, according to the grapevine, a bunch of doctors told Dee she couldn't get pregnant."

My heart hurt for Aaron's wife and child. "Thanks for telling me about him."

"You're welcome. It helps me process everything." Sheila dragged her feet through the water.

Aaron's shady past certainly made his death seem more and more like it could be murder—and not just an accident someone had tried to cover up.

After the flotilla parade was over and Sheila and Julian left, Laura and I floated in the water until we were prune-like and tired of the sun. When we climbed out of the lake, I wrapped a towel around my waist and set my raft on Laura's wagon.

She picked up her phone and furrowed her brow before looking up. "I heard from my friend at the coroner's office. The autopsy's done, and I'm only telling you this because it's being released to the public."

"Aaron was murdered?"

She nodded. "His death's officially been ruled a homicide."

CHAPTER SIX

"Is there anything else you're allowed to tell me about Aaron?" I asked Laura as I took the wagon handle and trudged toward her house. We'd been out of the water less than five minutes, and sweat was already trickling down my back.

"The warm water accelerated the gas formation in his body, which allowed his corpse to float to the surface pretty quickly," she said. "They're estimating Aaron's body went into the water sometime between Thursday night and early Friday morning. Cause of death was a blow to the head, and his skull was fractured."

I considered his running shoes. "Did someone hit him with a car?"

"No. But it appears Aaron may have fallen because he had minor scrapes on his knee and hand. Someone hit the side of his head with a heavy object like a baseball bat."

"Anything else?"

"That's all I know, but in light of this new information, I'd like you to contact Ryan McCloud and tell him everything you witnessed at Lachlan's Lighthouse." Laura squeezed water from her hair.

"Sure."

We plodded forward, the only sounds were the rumble of the wagon against asphalt and the rhythmic clips of our flip-flops. Her phone dinged again, and she glanced at it.

"About this afternoon and evening," she said. "Tommy's coming over, and we'll take the boat out. After dinner, we've been invited to Byron and Minnie Collins's house to watch the fireworks and have ice cream."

"He's the mayor of Hidden Shores, right?"

"Yes. They have a perfect view of the show from their pier."

"Sounds fun." When I was growing up, the annual fireworks display had been one of the highlights of my summer, and Lake Hideaway's show was always the Saturday after the July Fourth holiday.

"Tommy's . . . bringing a guest."

My heart kerthunked at her cautious tone. Surely, she wasn't trying to fix me up. Was that why she'd made negative comments about Hamlet earlier? "Who's that?" I managed to sound cool in spite of the inner freak out session happening in my brain.

"His five-year-old daughter Zenith."

I blinked. Hadn't seen that coming. "I didn't realize he had a daughter." And for the record, I would've only been surprised by the girl's name if I hadn't already met Tommy.

"She lives with her mother."

"I see."

"Tommy's ex-girlfriend, Nora Sutcliffe. Aaron Lehman's sister-in-law."

"Uh-huh."

"You're judging him."

"No, I'm not." I was twenty kinds of relieved she wasn't setting me up with a Tommy clone.

"Yes, you are."

Because Laura had her back to me, I rolled my eyes. "I haven't said a word other than to express my surprise that he has offspring." I stopped in her driveway and waited for her to open the garage door.

"*Offspring?*" She punched in the code, and the door lifted. "You've seriously got to dump Hamlet. You're starting to talk like him." She stomped between her boat trailer and Camaro.

Why was that such a bad thing? Hamlet was well read and intelligent. Then I remembered my truce with Laura and bit back a retort. "Tell me about Zenith."

"She's cute, and Tommy adores her. He's an awesome father."

Good to know there was at least one logical reason for Laura's attraction to him.

"He wishes he could spend more time with her, but his ex-girlfriend doesn't always make that easy." She stretched out her flamingo-print beach towel on a wooden drying rack. "But since Nora's brother-in-law just died, she needs Tommy's help with Zenith—for now."

"Is Zenith upset about her uncle dying?"

"Tommy's not sure she truly understands. Right now, the goal is to keep her distracted and answer her questions in the simplest way possible."

"I'm glad she can hang out with us tonight. I'm sure she'll enjoy the fireworks and ice cream." I squeezed my hair one last time before spreading my towel over the rack and retreating to the guest room where I left a message for Detective McCloud.

"I want to ride the tube with Miss Georgia." Zenith stood on the boat seat and gazed at me with enormous brown eyes as Laura buckled her bright pink life jacket. "Will you go with me? Please?"

I stopped spraying sunscreen on my arm and surveyed the lake. Not only was traffic heavy, but the wind had picked up, and the gray water churned with whitecaps. Tommy had avoided Smith Bay, and we floated on the south end of the lake near the edge of Hidden Shores. A white-steepled chapel, a Victorian-inspired bed and breakfast, and a row of condominiums kept watch over the boaters.

"You don't have to, Georgia." Tommy attached the rope to the boat and shoved the yellow and blue tube into the water. "It's pretty rough out there, and I understand if you're not itching to get in the water after you found—"

Laura cleared her throat—loudly.

"I don't mind." I put the sunscreen can in the cupholder, and bracing myself as a wave rocked the boat, I slipped on a life jacket and secured the plastic clasps. The tube had two lounge seats, so maybe I wouldn't flop around too much. My thirty-one-year-old body couldn't handle the crazy way I'd ridden as a teenager—face down, my belly smacking the tube and my legs flouncing every which way.

"Thank you, Miss Georgia." Zenith beamed. With her short pigtails bobbing, she climbed over the edge of the boat and plunked back into one of the seats like she'd done it a thousand times. "Will you go fast, Daddy?" She kicked her legs.

"Only if it's okay with Miss Georgia."

I didn't miss the challenge in those words. "Oh, it's *definitely* okay." I stepped onto the platform and eased onto the seat next to Zenith, who was already bouncing up and down. I grasped a handle and shoved us away from the boat.

Tommy gunned the engine, and we flew over the roiling water. Zenith gave a thumbs up, and Tommy increased the boat's speed. I stifled groans and held on for dear life as he made zigzagging turns. Zenith screeched with delight.

My back would be sore tomorrow.

Tommy plowed through a massive whitecap, and the tube went airborne before flicking us into the lake. When I resurfaced, I snorted water from my nose and scanned for dead bodies—just in case the Webster County mafia had decided to use the lake as a dumping ground.

When I was satisfied the area was clear, I swam to Zenith while keeping an eye out for wayward boats.

"You all right?" I swiped water from my eyes.

"Yes. But I have to go to the bathroom."

I flailed my arms and put some distance between us. "Go ahead."

Her pigtails flipped from side to side. "No, Miss Georgia. Number two."

Tommy stopped the boat next to us and cut the engine.

"We need to make a pit stop," I yelled.

The closest public restroom was located at Sutcliffe Marina, and after Tommy docked Laura's boat, we filed up the narrow pier toward the sprawling blue metal building that had been there as long as I could remember. Weeds tangled with the overgrown landscaping. Inside, rusty stains blotted ceiling tiles, and the concrete floors displayed narrow cracks. Red, white, and blue balloons wiggled next to a banner announcing a Fourth of July Sale.

"Daddy, can I have candy?" Zenith pointed to the check-out counter and gave Tommy a five-going-on-fifteen grin.

"Sure thing, sweetheart." As Laura escorted Zenith to the restroom, Tommy looked between the teenage boy behind the counter and me. "I'm a sucker. I'll cop to it." He opened his wallet.

I chuckled. I'd forgotten that in addition to selling boats, parts, and gas, the marina peddled dollar grab bags of assorted candy. No doubt the sneaky Miss Zenith had an ulterior motive for this stop at her family's marina.

While Tommy purchased a treat, I hummed along to "God Bless the U.S.A." playing on the radio and admired the expensive ski boats placed around the showroom. I homed in on a cobalt and white model with a shiny wakeboard tower and marched up metal steps arranged next to the boat. Peering inside, I ran my hand over the gleaming fiberglass.

"Good afternoon, ma'am." A red-headed, thirty-something man in a belly-defining polo wandered out of his office. "You in the market for a new boat?" His salesman-at-work expression was pleasant but almost too eager.

I climbed off the platform and patted the boat's hull. "I wish. She's beautiful." I motioned toward Tommy, who was at the cash register. "I'm with him and his girlfriend."

The man's friendly expression took a hike. With his tummy jiggling and nostrils flaring, he stomped over to Tommy. "Tommy Ferraro! I told you never to come here again!" The man's face grew mottled, and the light caught his flying spittle.

I hoped Zenith would take her sweet old time in the restroom.

Tommy turned from the register and didn't so much as flinch. "Hey, Craig."

Craig lunged in front of Tommy, blocking his path to the door. "What do you have to say for yourself?"

"If you want me to leave, step aside, and I'll be on my way."

Craig didn't budge and called Tommy a few choice words. To my surprise, Tommy's only reaction was crossing his arms—almost as if he were bored.

The teenage kid behind the counter took several steps back and plastered himself against the wall.

"I'll have you arrested for trespassing." Craig yanked his phone from his pocket.

"Seeing as how your father and I have a cordial relationship, you're not going to get very far." To Tommy's credit, he didn't smirk but delivered this information in a matter-of-fact tone.

Craig reared back and threw a punch, but Tommy jumped aside. Craig's fist met air, and he stumbled forward before catching himself on the counter. Whipping around, he held his hands in a fighting stance. His gut popped out of his polo.

"Uncle Craig!" Zenith ran ahead of Laura.

Uncle Craig?

"Hey, sweetie!" Craig dropped his arms and tucked in his shirt. "I didn't see you come in." He emitted a nervous chuckle. "Your dad and I were just messing around. Right, man?"

"Yep." Tommy's jaw ticked.

Craig must be Nora—and Dee's—brother. And if that was the case, why was he working instead of mourning his brother-in-law with his family? Were they short staffed? Extra busy because of the holiday weekend?

Zenith threw her arms around her uncle's ample waist. "Daddy's buying me candy."

"Is that right?" He patted her head. "What have you been up to?"

"Miss Georgia went tubing with me." She pointed at me.

Craig straightened and surveyed me with a generous dose of suspicion in his eyes. "I see."

Laura looked back and forth between Tommy and Craig.

Tommy swiped the candy bag from the counter, handed it to his daughter, and grasped her other hand. "See ya later, Craig. And for the record, I'm sorry about Aaron."

"Thanks." Craig fled to his office and slammed the door.

When Sheila had said the steamy weather was making people aggressive, she hadn't been kidding.

Once we were back on the boat, and Zenith was on the tube, I moved to a seat closer to Laura and Tommy. "What happened back there?" I yelled over the motor.

"Yeah," Laura shouted. "Zenith and I walked in on something."

As Tommy took Zenith for a ride, he gave Laura a quick summary of what she'd missed. "That lunatic can't get over the fact that I never married his sister when she got pregnant with Zenith," Tommy said. "It doesn't matter to him that I proposed, but Nora didn't accept. It's all my fault." He slapped his fuzzy chest.

"He's always been there for Zenith and paid support, and Nora's parents haven't held a grudge." Laura rested a hand on his arm.

In spite of my initial feelings about Tommy, I believed he was telling the truth, because it was pretty obvious that he adored his daughter. But I had a sense that I wasn't getting the full story. Craig's rage seemed out of proportion with something that'd happened over five years ago. "Why does he think he can ban you?"

Tommy snorted. "Now that his dad's retired, he's on a power trip running the place. I bought my Sea-Doo there a couple of years ago, and Mr. Sutcliffe's a member at the country club. Craig ain't gonna tell me I can't do business at that marina with my baby girl's family." His eyes darkened. "No way."

When we returned to Laura's house, I went upstairs to change and decided to try to call Hamlet, since I'd be busy the rest of the evening. I wasn't sure I'd be able to reach him, because he hated carrying his cellphone.

"Look at you all tan and beautiful," Hamlet said when he answered my video chat.

Tan was a bit of a stretch, but I'd roll with the compliment. "And windblown." I dropped on the bed and smoothed my damp hair. "How are rehearsals?"

"Everything's coming together nicely. Did I tell you the actress playing Marian is a friend of mine that I worked with in Chicago a few years ago?"

I squeezed the life out of a throw pillow as I arranged it behind my back. "No."

"She gets my humor, and she's rather quirky herself. It's a kick working with her again."

More like a kick in the pants. My stomach flipped. I was over-reacting. After all, she could be a married woman, but since there was no graceful way to ask without sounding like a jealous girl-friend, it was time for a subject change. "Have you found any new houses to flip?"

"I'm taking a break from that for now, so I can focus on the musical."

"I see." I was beginning to regret my decision to video chat because I was having an awfully hard time getting my facial expressions to behave.

"I finished the renovation on Detective Perkins's kitchen. It turned out well. Have him send you pictures."

"You don't have your own?" I battled a rogue frown. "Don't you want them for your website?" When he wasn't flipping houses, he took on renovation projects and had been talking about creating a website for potential clients. Apparently, the operative words were *had been*.

"Excellent idea." He snapped his fingers. "I should've thought of that. I'll contact Cal and ask him to send me some shots. Thank you." He waved a hand. "How's your visit with Laura going?"

I'd fully intended to tell Hamlet all about finding Aaron Lehman's body because I needed to get it off my chest, and part of me hoped the information would motivate him to rush up here and protect me. But now I wasn't so sure he'd come through, and I wasn't ready to handle that disappointment.

I swallowed over the growing lump in my throat. "Being here is bringing back so many great memories of Grandma and Grandpa Smith, and Laura's boyfriend Tommy has the cutest little girl named Zenith."

All true statements, right?

CHAPTER SEVEN

"How can I help?" I asked Laura when I went downstairs to the kitchen after talking to Hamlet. In the backyard, Tommy manned the grill on the patio while Zenith chased Gus, who was loving the attention.

"Just relax. Tommy's grilling marinated flank steak and vegetables." She pointed to the stove. "I already have the rice cooking and the fruit salad finished, so we're good to go."

I nodded.

She leaned against the marble counter and studied me. "I was expecting a smart aleck comment about your lack of culinary skills. Are you okay? I know I've been unsettled all day."

"Yeah. Finding a body wasn't exactly how I planned to start my vacation, and knowing Aaron was murdered makes it even worse." I went to the refrigerator and filled a glass with water. "I talked to Hamlet, so that helps." At least it should've helped. Maybe if I told myself it did, I'd believe it.

"If you want to invite him for the rest of the weekend, he's more than welcome." She twisted the fringe on her tank top. "I shouldn't have been so hard on him earlier. He's a fun guy. He'll cheer us all up."

I appreciated her positive words. "He's busy with rehearsals, so I don't think it's going to work out." I took a drink. "Thank you, though."

We walked out to the patio, and Zenith was playing catch with Gus in the grass in front of the channel.

"What's going on, ladies?" Tommy turned from the grill with tongs in hand.

"Just talking about Aaron." Laura donned her sunglasses and relaxed in an Adirondack chair made from vintage water skis. "The whole situation's tragic."

Next door, Keith and Rachel's house was quiet. Had Keith been able to find his wife to tell her about Aaron?

Tommy flipped the flank steak. "I've been thinking about who'd want to off him."

Laura and I glanced toward Zenith, but she was still oblivious because Gus was running after a rope toy she'd tossed.

"Do you have an idea?" I asked.

"You betcha." He turned from the grill and faced me. "Craig Sutcliffe."

I eased into the other Adirondack chair next to Laura. "No offense, but are you sure your bad relationship with him isn't clouding your judgment?"

Laura narrowed her eyes, which I did my best to ignore since I'd asked a legitimate question.

"None taken, sweetheart. It's a fair question, and that's why you're good at solving mysteries." Tommy pointed the tongs at me. "But I've got a story to back it up. Craig plays golf at the country club all the time, and about a month ago, I walked into the locker room. He was jawing with one of his buddies about how he suspected his brother-in-law was stepping out on Dee, and if he found out it was true, he was gonna kill Aaron with his bare hands."

Or a with a golf club.

When Tommy turned back to the grill, I glanced at Laura, and she shook her head, ever so slightly.

"It could be an idle threat from a guy with a short fuse." She crossed her thin legs. "But I'll pass along the information to Detective McCloud." She took her phone from her pocket, and her thumbs tapped the device.

"It's weird Craig was working when his brother-in-law just died," I said. "Why wasn't he comforting his sister?"

"Craig and Dee have always fought like cats and dogs, so maybe it's better if he stays outta her way," Tommy said. "Plus, I heard Sutcliffe Marina has been losing business the past few years, so they could've cut back on staff. Or . . . he's the type who grieves by keeping busy."

Though it was charitable of Tommy to tack on that last statement, I wasn't sure that was the case, and Tommy didn't seem convinced either. "If he's grieving Aaron at all."

"True," Tommy said. "I ain't good at this whole sleuthing business, but I want to see justice served, so I thought I'd better pipe up. Aaron Lehman didn't deserve to die like that."

I considered my own daddy's murder that'd gone unsolved for nearly a decade and how painful it'd been living without answers. Even now, the experience motivated me to find answers for victims' families. "You're right. No one does."

We grew quiet and watched an elderly man and woman on a pontoon boat pass by on the channel.

A door slammed, and Sheila—without Pickles—scurried into Laura's yard. "I'm glad you're home. I need to talk to Georgia."

Laura and I exchanged glances.

"What's going on?" I stood.

"First off, I was poking around online when I came across

some information about you." Sheila put her hands on her ample hips. "Why didn't you tell me you're a detective?"

"I'm not." Why was she researching me? "I'm a farmer who's helped my local sheriff's department with a few investigations."

Sheila eyed me as if I'd been a part of a nefarious plot designed to deceive her—and *only* her. "And one of those investigations brought you here to Webster County. Seems you might've mentioned that when you were talking to me about Aaron. I wondered why you asked so many questions."

Laura ducked her head, and Tommy had his back to us trying to look busy, but I spotted his smirk in the window's reflection as he lifted the flank steak onto a plate and covered it with foil.

"I'm sorry. I wasn't trying to hide anything," I said.

"Never mind. What's done is done. My son needs your help." She tapped her foot against the cement. "That head-in-the-clouds detective thinks my Keith killed Aaron."

I hadn't seen that one coming. "Really?" I sneaked a peek at Zenith, who was still entertaining Gus.

"The cops got a hold of Aaron's text messages, and my son was supposed to meet Aaron the night he was killed," she said.

I glanced at Tommy and Laura who looked as surprised as I felt. "Why?"

"Allegedly, Keith was warning people about taking their boats to Sutcliffe Marina because he was seeing boats with issues after they'd been serviced there."

Is that why Sutcliffe had been losing business? Even though Aaron's in-laws owned that marina, I struggled to make the connection to his murder. "Aaron didn't work at Sutcliffe Marina, did he?"

"Not yet." Sheila swatted a fly. "But I heard that he had somehow talked his father-in-law Don into handing him the keys to the kingdom when he finished his management degree because Craig was doing such a lousy job running the place."

I didn't dare look at Laura or Tommy because the potential of losing his job to Aaron would be a perfect motive for Craig, and the marina did appear rundown.

Tommy coughed, but Sheila didn't appear to notice.

"Don caught wind of what Keith was saying and asked Aaron to speak to Keith," she said. "Maybe Don even saw it as a test of Aaron's management skills. Or thought Keith would listen to his wife's favorite cousin, and they could resolve the issue peacefully before Don got lawyers involved. Bottom line is, Aaron and Keith agreed to meet on Thursday night to discuss the problems, and now the cops are accusing my baby."

That timeframe certainly gave Keith opportunity since Aaron had been killed late Thursday night or early Friday morning, but from what I could see, Craig had a stronger motive.

"Would Keith lie to give your business an advantage over your competitors?" Laura asked.

"My son's not a liar. He knows shoddy work when he sees it, and he wasn't afraid to tell Aaron the truth," Sheila snapped. "Besides, if Keith was lying to get ahead, wouldn't he have been spreading rumors about Hideaway Marina too?"

"Good point," I said.

Sheila lifted her chin. "My husband founded Thurston's Marina, and he always prided himself on providing excellent customer service—and Keith has done his best to carry on that tradition."

"Which he has." Laura offered Sheila a reassuring smile. "I've been pleased with my new boat."

Sheila glared at my friend with such intensity that Tommy tightened his grip on the tongs and looked ready to pounce.

"I take it Keith doesn't have an alibi?" I asked quickly.

"No." Sheila shuffled her feet. "Rachel was working, and Julian was with me because Keith said he needed to run out for groceries. I offered to let Julian sleep over."

He *had* lied to his mother about why he'd needed a babysitter, but maybe Keith hadn't shared the real reason because he hadn't wanted her to worry about the business.

Or he truly was lying to cover his tracks, and Mama Bear Sheila couldn't see it. But what if Tommy was right about Craig, and Keith *was* being falsely accused? Craig could've pointed Detective McCloud to Keith to take the heat off of himself.

"Will you help?" Sheila pressed her hands together. "Please? Think of Julian. He's already been through so much with his parents' marriage drama."

Tommy and Laura exchanged glances.

I was already involved whether I liked it or not. So much for a relaxing vacation. "I'll do what I can, but I have to warn you. My advantage at home is that a lot of people know me and are willing to talk because my family's lived in Wildcat Springs for several generations. Around here, I'm just another strange laker, so I might not get much information."

Sheila waved a hand. "Leave that to me. I've lived here since I was born and go to the biggest church in town. I'll put in a good word for you."

Mayor Byron Collins and his wife Minnie lived in one of the million-dollar homes that I'd grown up admiring from afar. The kind of lakefront property that, when it went on sale, was only open to showings for qualified buyers. I wasn't poor, but I'd certainly never meet that criterion, so I'd always had to satisfy my curiosity by looking at pictures in online real estate listings.

It was after nine o'clock when Laura, Tommy, Zenith, and I arrived, and the sun was setting. Because of daylight saving time, the fireworks wouldn't start until after ten. I hoped Zenith could stay awake, because she appeared zombie-like as Laura led her toward the two-story house with red siding and stone accents that gave it a Craftsman vibe.

Zenith turned to me and pointed at the brick monstrosity next door. "My mamaw and papaw live in that house."

"I see." The house was dark. Had they gathered at their daughter's home? "I bet you have fun swimming here, don't you?"

"Uh-huh. They have a big raft with a trampoline," Zenith said.

When Mayor and Mrs. Collins greeted us at the door, Tommy made introductions, and they insisted I call them Byron and Minnie. She was hollow-cheeked and thin but attractive, and he was prematurely gray but handsome. I guessed they were both in their early forties. Both were barefoot and wearing jeans with matching patriotic T-shirts.

Tommy put his arm around Minnie. "Byron and Minnie made me feel at home when I moved here and didn't know anybody."

"Aww. We like having you around." She leaned her head against his shoulder. "We think Zenith is pretty special too." She held open her arms, and Zenith ran and hugged her. "I have ice cream."

Zenith's face lit up, and she looked at Tommy. "Can I have some, Daddy?"

"Sure thing, Z."

Minnie led us into the open-concept kitchen, living room, and dining room that faced two-story windows with a lake view. A large family picture of Byron, Minnie, and a little girl hung over the fireplace. The photo didn't look like it'd been taken all that long ago. Where was their daughter?

"Make yourselves comfortable. I set out the fixings for sundaes." Minnie pointed to the island. It held so many varieties of ice cream toppings that it looked like one of those frozen yogurt shops where it was way too easy to spend six or seven bucks on a single cup.

That might or might not've happened to me on a date—or two —back in the day and probably went a long way in explaining my unwed state.

"Please, don't be shy." Minnie handed us red plastic bowls and flag-print napkins.

No worries.

I chose mint chocolate chip ice cream, fudge, and crushed Oreos for a topping. We took our dessert out to the pier where chairs were arranged at the end, and white string lights were draped along the metal posts. While we ate our ice cream and talked about crops, the weather, and Minnie and Byron's plans to take a river cruise through Europe later in the month, the sky grew darker. Around the lake, the occasional firecracker sparkled as people lit their own.

Gus had done such a great job of wearing Zenith out that not even the sugar affected her, and she dozed in Minnie's lap.

"Is it true you were the ones who found Aaron Lehman this morning?" Minnie looked at Laura, Tommy, and me as she stroked Zenith's hair.

"Sure is." Tommy glanced at his daughter.

Laura tugged her sweatshirt sleeves over her hands. "Georgia literally bumped into his body in the water."

Byron cringed. "I'm so sorry."

Minnie shivered and directed her concerned gaze at me. "Do you need more ice cream?" Her face was completely serious.

A whole tub of mint chocolate chip and a spoon, please. "No, other than feeling sad for the family, I'm fine. Thank you, though."

Byron collected our empty bowls. "Aaron worked for my company a few years back—before I was elected mayor. I always liked him."

"Byron worked in the RV manufacturing industry." Minnie looked at me.

I appreciated her clarification. "What was Aaron like?" Might as well sniff around.

"A hard worker and a good leader. He'd served time for dealing drugs and was determined to change his life when he came to work for me," Byron said. "Took up with some of the Amish men who worked in the factory. For a while, the scuttlebutt was that he might become Amish, but he never followed through."

"Interesting." Northern Indiana had a large Amish population, and it wasn't unusual for some Amish men to get manufacturing jobs to help support their families if farming wasn't an option. Living a lifestyle devoid of many modern conveniences like automobiles and electricity would take a serious commitment, so I wasn't surprised Aaron had bailed.

"That would be a major adjustment," Laura said.

Tommy chuckled. "I sure couldn't live that way."

I tried to picture Tommy in suspenders—and without his gold-chain necklace—and just couldn't get there. *Nice Georgia.* I focused before a giggle escaped. "Did you ever hear what changed Aaron's mind?"

"He met the Sutcliffe girl, and they got married," Byron said. "One of the guys told me Aaron thought he needed to get a college degree, so he quit his job at the plant and was studying management part time at a college in Fort Wayne while he worked at Lachlan's."

Had Aaron felt like he didn't measure up to Dee's family's expectations without a college education? Or had he simply wanted to provide a better life for his family? "Did Aaron get along with his in-laws?"

Byron and Minnie glanced at each other. "Let's just say Don and Caterina tolerated him for Dee's sake, but he never would've been their first choice for her," Minnie said. "Still, they're very excited for their new grandbaby." She looked toward the Sutcliffes' darkened house.

Not exactly a glowing endorsement. "Is it true that Don was thinking about having Aaron take over the marina?"

"I'm not sure Don's tolerance goes that far," Byron said. "Why all the questions?"

I decided to be honest with them. "I sort of have a little sleuthing hobby."

"And you're trying to figure out what happened to—*achoo!*" Minnie withdrew a tissue from her pocket and dabbed her nose while Zenith still snoozed.

"Bless you," Tommy said.

"Thanks. Stupid allergies." She sniffed.

"Georgia's already managed to get some good intel." Laura zipped her sweatshirt. "Even without my help."

"Good. I don't want people feeling like our town is unsafe." Byron's forehead crinkled. "I can't think of anything else, but if I do—or hear anything—I'll let you know."

Byron had already given me a lead without realizing it. "Do you think Aaron's Amish friends from the RV plant might talk to me?"

Byron gazed at the water. "Moses Zook might. He and Aaron ate lunch together all the time."

I leaned forward. "Would you mind asking if I can speak with him?"

"I'd be happy to. He's pretty reserved, but if I joined you, I'm sure he wouldn't mind at all, given what happened to his friend."

"Thanks." I wasn't sure how I felt about Byron tagging along, but I wasn't going to complain.

A streaky blue and white firework streamed downward like a weeping willow, and a boom thundered across the lake, echoing off the seawalls. Zenith lifted her head and squinted at the sky, where a large green smiley face grinned at us.

I'd worry about the case later. Right now it was time to enjoy the show.

The next morning, Laura, Gus, and I opted to attend Boat-in Worship on the shore of Hideaway Retreat Center. Every Sunday morning between Memorial Day and Labor Day, the area churches put on a weekly service, and the local pastors took turns preaching.

Laura let me drive her boat across the lake, but I surrendered captain duties when we approached the mass of about fifty boats anchored along the shore. A crowd had gathered in the lawn in front of the stone building, and folks sat on blankets and in lawn chairs. The morning was sunny, but hazy, promising another day of heat and humidity.

She maneuvered by the retreat center's main pier, and we picked up a couple of bulletins from a man in a fishing hat before she navigated along the outer edge of the cluster of boats.

"A few weeks ago, I learned the hard way, you don't want to get into that mess—especially when there's a good breeze." She cut the engine.

We could still hear a guitarist playing "Amazing Grace" clearly. Byron and Minnie, also anchored well outside the fray, waved at us. They'd named their speed boat *Minnie Happy Returns*.

Without Tommy's assistance, Laura and I managed to anchor —even with the wind. For fear of violating our truce, I hadn't asked why Tommy wasn't joining us, and Laura hadn't offered the information. I figured he had to golf with some semi-famous people.

Nice Georgia.

We stretched out in the bow and sipped coffee from travel mugs, and I tried not to move too much because my legs and arms were sore from skiing. Gus lay between us, gnawing on his life jacket strap. This was his first time at church, so I hoped he'd behave. The guitarist finished playing, and a men's quartet sang "How Great Thou Art."

When the song was over, the congregation applauded, and the pastor opened with prayer and preached a sermon on trusting God to be our refuge and to work in our circumstances. Considering my confusion about my relationship with Hamlet, it was a message I needed to hear.

Help me trust you, Lord. Help me to want what you want—and please show me what that is.

As the men's quartet closed with "I'll Fly Away," I spotted Byron tugging the anchor, and a gust of wind pushed their boat toward the middle of the lake. They must be in a hurry.

Laura followed my gaze. "They're always rushing to beat the Sunday brunch crowd to the country club."

Byron slid into the driver's seat and tried to start the boat—but it stalled. "Come on!" He slammed his palm against the steering wheel.

"Shhh!" Minnie scowled as he tried again.

But the engine wouldn't come to life, and they continued to drift. The quartet landed on their final notes, and the congregation applauded.

One second later, *Minnie Happy Returns* exploded.

CHAPTER EIGHT

Gus barked as black smoke billowed into the thick air and debris rained into the water. Laura and I shot to our feet, and I blinked, trying to process what'd happened. Several people screamed. With arms flailing, Minnie bobbed in the water and tried to reach a floating red cushion. I couldn't see Byron.

"Help!" Minnie screeched.

In one motion, I swiped a life vest and shoved my arms in as I jumped overboard—with Gus at my side.

Great. I hadn't expected my canine companion to launch himself in the water. But I should've.

"Where's Byron?" Minnie slapped her arms against the water and coughed.

With Gus paddling next to me, I ignored my sore muscles and swam toward the wreckage. Byron was floating near what remained of the sinking bow. "I see him!"

"Get him, and I'll help Minnie." Laura swam next to me.

I hadn't even realized she'd followed me. I reached Byron as he grasped a piece of the wreckage. Pushing aside a boat fender, I grabbed him around the waist and hauled him toward Laura's boat while Gus paddled with us. Byron's left arm was red and raw, and a jagged cut marred his cheekbone. "Laura's got Minnie."

"Thank you," he whispered.

A pontoon approached, and a middle-aged woman in a visor held up her phone. "I called 9-1-1." She stopped the boat, and recognition dawned on her face. "Oh my! Mayor Collins?" She opened the gate, dropped the ladder with a splash, and reached out her hand.

"Yes, ma'am. I can climb up. Thank you." Grimacing, Byron grasped the ladder and glanced over his shoulder at Laura and Minnie. Then he dragged himself aboard. When he staggered forward, Visor Lady steadied him, handed him a towel, and helped him to a seat.

I caught Gus and floated to the side of the boat in case I needed to boost Minnie out of the water.

Minnie reached for the ladder, and Visor Lady lugged her on board. Other than a few small cuts, Minnie appeared uninjured, and she fell into her husband's arms, sobbing.

Sirens howled as the ambulance drew closer.

"Let's get you to that ambulance." Visor Lady handed Minnie a towel and looked down at us in the water. "You gals coming?"

Laura hitched her thumb toward her boat. "We'll meet you on shore."

A while later, Laura, Gus and I huddled on shore in front of the retreat center, introduced ourselves to Jane the Visor Lady, and watched the ambulance transporting Byron and Minnie leave the parking lot. Many of the churchgoers stood in clusters and pointed toward the debris on the lake.

Jane wrapped her arms around her waist. "What could've

caused their boat to explode?" She looked back and forth at us. "Boats just don't blow up like that."

"Actually," Laura said. "It's more common than you think. If a boat's been sitting, sometimes gas fumes build up in the bilge, and if there's a spark . . ."

"Byron should've run the blower for several minutes before starting the engine, but they were in a hurry," I said.

Life Lesson #12,001: Never skip out on church to beat the brunch crowd.

I gazed out at the remains of the boat, now surrounded by a couple of speedboats from the sheriff's department. "My grandpa always took the extra precaution of lifting the engine cover even before running the blower."

Jane's eyes widened. "I had no idea. I reckon my husband and I need to read about boating safety. We're new to this lake thing—he's playing tennis this morning." She adjusted her visor. "He'll be ticked he missed the excitement."

Merciful heavens. I fought an oncoming burst of laughter. "Thanks for helping us out today."

"My pleasure." Jane tightened her grip on her boat keys and glanced toward the lake. "I sure hope what happened today was an accident like you say, but my sixth sense is tingling—especially since the mayor's involved."

I wrapped Gus's leash around my hand. Now that Jane mentioned her sixth sense, mine was going crazy too.

Laura and I returned to her house, and she whipped up a batch of blueberry pancakes for brunch. I offered to help, but she knew better than to accept because it was safer for all concerned if I refrained from food preparation. After I set the table on her screened-in porch, I sat at the peninsula, sipped coffee, and watched her work while Gus lay on the tile at my feet.

"What if the explosion wasn't an accident?" I leaned my elbows against the countertop and clutched the mug with both hands.

She finished stirring, set the bowl aside, and looked me straight in the eye. "Byron didn't run the blower. Not to mention, there could've been a leak in the boat's fuel line. Don't go looking for another mystery."

I didn't have to go looking for mysteries when they so easily found me. But another detail was bugging me—big time. "Keith Thurston reported poor work coming out of Sutcliffe Marina. What if Byron and Minnie had their boat serviced there since their neighbors own the place?"

"We don't know that." She poured batter on the griddle.

"If someone there did substandard work, it could prove Keith was justified in warning people not to take their boats to Sutcliffe."

"Byron and Minnie could've had their boat serviced at Thurston's or Hideaway Marina—or Byron might've tinkered with it himself." She reached over and stirred the blueberry sauce.

"Is he mechanically inclined?"

"I don't know. Ask Tommy."

My mind swirled with more scenarios. "What if Byron and Minnie had their boat serviced at Thurston's Marina, but Craig snuck over to their house and sabotaged the fuel line to discredit Keith and *his* marina?"

"That's pretty far-fetched."

"If Craig killed Aaron, we already know he's desperate."

"True."

"What if someone has it out for Byron because he's the

mayor?" I set the mug aside. "Has Byron caused any controversies?"

"No. He's well-liked as far as I can tell. But then, I've not lived here that long." She removed a spatula from a drawer. "God was watching out for them both. The explosion could've been tragic."

I remembered the family photo with the little girl. "Speaking of tragedies, did Byron and Minnie lose a child?"

"Yes. I saw you looking at the photo above their mantel last night, and I was praying you wouldn't say anything." She flipped the pancakes. "Their daughter Avery died of leukemia about four years ago. That's why Minnie makes over Zenith so much." She picked up a platter. "Let's eat, and then I'll give Ryan McCloud a call and see what I can find out about the explosion."

"Sounds good."

Her phone dinged, and she peeked at it. "So I did something you might not like."

You agreed to marry Tommy? I shoved the thought away and bit my tongue before it went rogue, and I said the words aloud. "What's that?"

"When you were in the bathroom this morning before church, I got Hamlet's number from your phone, texted him, and asked him to come for the rest of the weekend."

My stomach tightened. "Let me guess. He turned you down because of musical rehearsals."

"No." Her forehead creased with concern. "He's on his way and will be here in an hour or so."

The tension left my stomach, and I sat up straighter. "Oh." *Way to tip your hand, Georgia Rae.* I thought of the morning's sermon. Maybe God had arranged this visit so I could have some clarification about my relationship with Hamlet. "Well then, thank you. I'll be glad to see him."

"Uh-huh." She slipped the pancakes from the griddle to a platter.

Apparently, I hadn't sold that very well, but I really *was* glad Hamlet was coming.

CHAPTER NINE

Laura and I knew better than to discuss the case on her porch, because we could never be sure if Sheila was lurking next door. Instead, we talked about the fireworks show and made quick work of the pancakes. While I cleaned the kitchen, she excused herself to her office to call Detective McCloud.

As I loaded the dishwasher, I thought about Hamlet's impending visit and what was bugging me about his return to theater. If he found joy acting in productions at Bell's Dinner Theater in Richardville, I had no problem supporting him. The trouble was, acting roles were limited in Central Indiana, and if he got the bug and pursued more opportunities, then there was no telling where he might land.

When we'd begun dating, he'd given me the impression he was ready to flip and renovate houses, marry, and start a family. But the whole time we'd been together, there'd been signs he missed acting. Vague comments. Not wanting to attend a community theater production when I'd made the suggestion. Talking about past productions.

He had the right to change his mind, and I certainly didn't want to hold him back from his dreams—wherever they took him. But I couldn't relocate because my profession tied me to Wildcat Springs.

You could always be a music teacher.

I swatted the stray thought like an annoying gnat and shut the dishwasher. Student teaching had shown me that my love of music didn't transfer to instructing squirmy children and attitude-infested adolescents. I'd spent months agonizing over what to do with my life.

When Grandpa Winston talked about selling our farm after Daddy died, I knew what needed to happen. Farming was what I'd been meant to do all along.

And I loved every part of it. Working the ground. Planting. Spraying. Harvesting. Hauling grain. I didn't even mind the business aspects of creating crop plans, managing finances, and prepping for taxes.

I squirted dish soap in the sink and turned on the water.

If I'd quit, Grandpa would be forced to retire even though he claimed he wanted to work until he died. Sure we'd hang onto some land and cash rent it to other farmers to have extra income, but once we sold our equipment and most of the land, there'd be no turning back. The cost to restart would be astronomical.

Blueberry pancakes sloshed in my stomach as I slid the griddle into the water and scrubbed it.

If Hamlet pursued acting and we continued our relationship, then I could be faced with a major question. Did I love him enough to quit farming and become a teacher?

"Georgia, come into my office, please," Laura yelled a few minutes after I'd finished drying the breakfast dishes.

Her office was near the front door. I wasn't exactly the world's best housekeeper, but her workspace made my house look spick-and-span. Though the rest of her home was perfectly neat, this room was a dumping ground. Papers were strewn over her metal and glass desk. Books were stacked in piles placed around the room because the floor-to-ceiling shelves behind her desk were full.

I paused next to the French doors, and she motioned for me to enter. She rooted around in a closet cluttered with plastic storage totes, folding chairs, and a card table. She backed out, dragging a small whiteboard and stand with her. "Ryan told me I could share a few more things with you—mostly because he knows your history of helping the Richard County Sheriff's Department, but you have to keep the information to yourself." She opened the stand and set the board on it.

"No problem."

She pointed to the couch next to her desk and uncapped a green marker. "Get comfy."

Great minds really did think alike. If we'd been at my place, I would've put case details on the chalk wall painted in my dining room.

"According to all our witnesses, Aaron was last seen Thursday night when he closed Lachlan's. The employees cleaned up and left at the same time. Aaron turned right out of the parking lot and drove north on Lake Loop Road. Ryan confirmed what Sheila told us—that according to some text messages Aaron *was* supposed to meet Keith on Thursday night."

"Where?"

"Lakeview Park."

"Which is north of the restaurant and right off of Smith Bay." I leaned forward. "Has Keith been arrested?"

"No. What Sheila *didn't* tell us was that Keith cancelled and rescheduled his meeting with Aaron for Saturday afternoon, and there are text messages to prove it. Still, given the circumstances with the competing marinas, Ryan wanted to question Keith."

"But Keith doesn't have an alibi for Thursday night?"

"Oh no. He has an alibi." Laura giggled. "Instead of grocery shopping and staying at home alone, he was having a sleep study at a hospital in Fort Wayne and didn't want Sheila to know because she'd freak out with worry about his sleep apnea. The hospital confirmed he was wired for sound—all night."

"Good grief." I squeezed the bridge of my nose.

"I know, right?" Laura drew a line through Keith's name.

I stared at the board and realized there was a big piece I'd missed. "If Aaron's coworkers saw him leave and drive around Lake Loop Road, then what happened to his car? The one we saw at the park yesterday morning didn't belong to him."

"Deputies found Aaron's car at Thurston's Marina this morning. Nobody noticed because Thurston's has a big parking lot for the people who rent pier spaces."

I pictured the rows of boats docked at the marina, and there were plenty of folks who owned small cabin cruisers and spent entire weekends on the lake. "Aaron's killer put the car there, knowing it'd take a while for anyone to notice. Are there any security cameras in the parking lot?"

"No. They're all pointed at the boats."

"Convenient."

"Exactly."

Someone had to have known about the lack of cameras in order to take that chance. "I realize you probably can't tell me who, but does Detective McCloud have a prime suspect?"

"Ryan mentioned there are several people they still needed to talk to because of Aaron's past, but they're not ready to arrest anyone," Laura said.

"All right." I mulled over everything I'd learned and observed.

"What about Craig Sutcliffe? If his dad was going to hand the business over to Aaron, then Craig has a motive."

"Last night, I let Ryan know what Tommy overheard and what Sheila told us, so he's going to follow up." She wrote his name on the whiteboard. "After seeing Craig attack Tommy, I think it's certainly plausible Craig attacked Aaron before dumping him in the water." She faced me and tapped the marker against her hand. "Who else should I add?"

"The wife—Dee Sutcliffe Lehman."

Laura shook her head. "She has an alibi. Her mom had foot surgery on Thursday, and Dee was at her parents' house from the time the surgery was over until Friday around noon. Apparently, her dad is a horrible nurse, so she had to step in."

This also gave her parents alibis too. Unless. "Dee could've sneaked out without her parents knowing. Their house is huge, and her mom was probably taking pain medication."

"I suppose it's possible." She scribbled Dee's name on the board. "But how realistic is it that a very pregnant woman killed her husband and dumped his body in the lake?"

Laura had a point. "Not very. Unless she had help. Maybe she worked with Craig or her dad." I studied the board. "Yesterday at Lachlan's Lighthouse, Dee seemed convinced Aaron was having an affair, which would give her motive. Something Lachlan said made me think she could be right. He said, 'I don't even *know for a fact* if Aaron is having an affair.' Which means he may've witnessed something shady with Aaron and didn't want to tell Dee."

"Right. Because she was a frantic wife trying to find answers about her missing husband." Laura clearly enjoyed playing devil's advocate.

"Perhaps." I considered Dee's dramatic reaction, and something about it almost seemed over the top—like a performance. "What if it was an act?"

"It could've been. So we won't rule her out yet. Anyone else?"

"Lachlan. When he broke up the confrontation with Dee and Alexa, he seemed guilty. It could be because he'd heard about the body in the lake and didn't want to tell Dee what he suspected— or because he knew why Aaron was in the water in the first place."

Laura jotted down his name. "What would his motive be?"

"No idea. Aaron might've suspected Lachlan was doing something shady in his business, and he silenced Aaron before he could blow the whistle?" We didn't have any evidence of that, but it would be smart to talk to Lachlan.

"Is that it?" she asked.

I studied our notes. "Add the boat explosion. Just in case it's connected to the competing marinas."

"Sure." She scribbled *boat explosion?* on the board.

A vehicle door slammed.

Capping the marker, Laura glanced out the window. "Your boyfriend's here. I'll make myself scarce so you can give him an appropriate greeting." She waggled her eyebrows and slipped out of her office.

My face flamed as I swung open the front door. "Hey."

Hamlet dropped his duffel bag on the sidewalk and kissed me with so much enthusiasm that I wondered why I'd been worried about his devotion.

When the kiss ended, I gazed into his handsome face. "I guess you missed me."

"Why would you think otherwise, Georgia Rae?" Concern flitted through his expression.

"I don't know." I rested my hand on his chest. "Never mind. Come in. I have a lot to tell you." I grasped his hand and noted with satisfaction that Laura would have nothing to criticize about his clothing. He wore a perfectly normal pair of khaki shorts and a navy button-down shirt with a tiny pineapple print.

Laura joined Hamlet and me in the living room as I told him about finding Aaron Lehman's body and learning that he'd been murdered. I relayed the story of Byron and Minnie's boat explosion but didn't say anything about the details Laura had shared.

When I finished, Hamlet smiled at Laura. "It's clear you invited me so I could help keep Georgia out of trouble."

"That may've been in the back of my mind, but I thought you'd enjoy some time away," she said.

In spite of criticizing him the day before, she seemed sincere.

"I will, though I'll have to go home tomorrow for some evening rehearsals," he said.

"Then we'll have to make the most of our time." Laura stood. "Let's take the boat out. Tommy has to work all day and won't be here until supper."

"I'll go change." Hamlet grabbed his duffel bag and dashed out of the room.

"I got a text from Byron Collins," Laura said. "He and Minnie have been treated and released from the hospital."

"Oh good."

"Other than cuts and burns and feeling pretty shaken up, they're fine. He's still willing to meet with you and Moses Zook. He suggested breakfast tomorrow morning at Arlene's Café and Variety Store."

I'd been to that little place in Amish country with Grandma Smith a time or two, and the cinnamon rolls were legendary. "As long as Byron feels up to it."

"He wouldn't have offered if he didn't. I've got to work, but I'll let him know Hamlet will be joining you."

"Thanks." With the explosion, I'd forgotten about Moses and Aaron's friendship, and I hoped Moses would be able to give us some insight into Aaron's life.

"So this is where you found Aaron." Hamlet shaded his eyes and gazed out at Smith Bay as we idled in Laura's boat along the marsh's cattails. "What a tragic situation."

Unlike yesterday morning when we'd had the inlet to ourselves, today, there were plenty of boats and jet skis darting around.

"It is," I said. "He left behind a wife and unborn child."

A wave rocked Laura's boat, and I checked out Lakeview Park on the peninsula that separated Smith Bay from Calloway Cove. In addition to piers and a beach, the park contained a boat ramp—the lake's single public access point. "It's possible someone used the ramp at the park to launch a boat and dump Aaron's body, so the murderer might not even own property or rent a pier space."

"Good point," Laura said. "It's unlikely that someone used the beach to dump Aaron's body because the lake's too shallow, but I've seen the lake's depth charts, and the water's at least thirty feet in the middle of the bay."

Hamlet cringed. "The killer certainly could've taken care of business quickly."

We stood in silence, observing our surroundings. Until my stomach roared.

"Yikes." I pressed my hand against my tummy. "I'm thinking it's time to grab some lunch. How about we head over to Lachlan's Lighthouse?" I motioned toward Sunrise Point.

"I have a feeling you're after more than just lunch, Georgia Rae." Hamlet grinned.

"You know me well." I curled up in the back seat next to my boyfriend. "It's time we talk to Lachlan—and Alexa the server."

"Onward." Laura pulled back on the throttle, and we flew across the lake toward Lachlan's. When we arrived, she found a space at the crowded pier and slid her boat into the slot with impressive ease, once again proving she didn't need Tommy's assistance.

All the tables on the deck around the lighthouse were full, so we filed inside the main dining room where paintings of lighthouses decorated the paneled walls. I wasn't going to protest sitting in air conditioning on this sticky day, so we found an empty table next to the window.

Alexa trotted over and dealt cocktail napkins onto the table. "I'm Alexa, and I'll be . . ." She met my eyes. "You were here yesterday morning." She glanced at Laura and Hamlet. "But with a different guy."

"Yes," I said. "The food was so great we had to come back and bring *my* boyfriend this time."

Alexa dug an order pad out of her apron. "I apologize that I didn't finish taking care of you yesterday, but something happened, and I needed a minute, and then we found out that our bartender was murdered." She swallowed hard, and tears welled in her eyes. "So yesterday was pretty awful."

"No need to apologize," I said. "I'm sorry for your loss."

"Thanks."

"I saw that woman yelling at you. I was about ready to jump in when your boss showed up."

Alexa's face darkened. "All I ever did with her husband was make obscure references to *Friends* because we both loved the show. He was a great guy, but that's it. I have my own boyfriend. Aaron's wife seriously has a screw loose. For all she knew, I could be the kind to beat her to a pulp for coming at me like that. If she didn't have a bun in the oven, I'd have put her flat on her back."

Given the way Alexa had cowered against the wall, I wasn't convinced she was a black belt in disguise, but I couldn't let her see that. *Cue the slight head tilt, sympathetic squinty eyes, and slow nod.* "That would've been understandable." I hoped I appeared like I was buying what she was selling.

She pressed her lips together. "What can I get you?"

We placed our orders for Cokes and hamburgers with fries, and before Alexa left our table, I asked to speak with Lachlan.

A few minutes later, he emerged from the back hallway and headed for our table. "You wanted to see me?" He set our Cokes on the table and adjusted his Cubs cap.

"First," I said. "You have a great place. We had breakfast here yesterday, and I had to come back for lunch today."

He beamed and tossed three straws on the table. "Thanks."

"Yesterday, I was in the restroom when I overheard Dee Lehman accusing Alexa of having an affair with her husband, and since Aaron died—"

"Who are you?" Lachlan narrowed his eyes.

"Georgia Winston." *Farmer. Amateur sleuth. Unsuccessful vacationer.*

"She's the one who found Aaron in the water." Hamlet met Lachlan's gaze with an icy stare.

"Oh." He flinched. "You all good?"

I took a deep breath, and—full disclosure—it was partly for show. "I will be."

"If it makes you feel any better," Laura said, "My name is Laura Patterson, and I'm a deputy prosecutor here in Webster County."

Lachlan slid into the chair next to Laura. "What do you want to know?" He reached out and patted my hand.

"*Was* Aaron having an affair?" I asked.

Lachlan rested his elbow on the table and cupped his hand over his chin. "Honestly, I'm not sure. Coulda been. He was quite the charmer." He dropped his hand. "See, about six months ago, a pretty young gal shows up at the back door of this restaurant and asks for Aaron. Her mascara's all streaked, and she starts sobbing when I tell her he's busy. *Begs* me to go get him, so I march to the bar and tell Aaron to take care of the girl before she disturbs the few customers we've got."

"Then what happened?" I removed my straw from its wrapping and shoved it into my Coke.

"They step outside and talk about five minutes, even though it was about ten degrees and snowing. Aaron makes a call. Next thing I know, he's in here asking me for the rest of the night off. Says there's something he needs to take care of for his friend. I let him go. The next day he comes to work like normal."

"Did he ever say any more about it?"

"Next day, I ask if he got his friend taken care of, and he says everything's fine."

"Did he ask you not to say anything to Dee?" Hamlet asked.

Lachlan shook his head. "Never said a word about that. When Dee was so upset yesterday, I didn't have the heart to tell her about this incident—especially when I didn't have proof that Aaron was cheating. When she mentioned he was missing . . ." He squeezed the bridge of his nose. "I'd heard a man had been found in the lake and was wondering if it was Aaron, because even though he's sometimes a little late for work, he'd never blown us off completely. I just didn't want to make things worse for her."

That explained his body language the day before. "Did Aaron ever mention the girl's name?"

"Never asked, and he didn't say."

That figured. "What else can you tell us about the mystery girl?"

"Young—early twenties or so. Petite. Smoking hot."

His vague description could match a lot of girls in town. "Did any of your other employees see her?"

"Not that I know of. Business was slow that night because of the weather, so I sent a bunch of people home. I have a high turnover." He leaned back and crossed his arms over his chest. "Look, I told all this to Detective McCloud, but I'm not even sure it's important since it happened months ago, and Aaron never mentioned it again."

"You've been helpful." I wasn't sure how much more information I'd be able to get from Lachlan, but I had a feeling I needed to try. "What can you tell me about Dee Lehman?"

"She's a piece of work. I went to high school with her, and not much has changed." He rolled his eyes. "I know she lost her husband, but *Dee* puts the *D* in drama. If somebody made a reality TV show about the housewives of Lake Hideaway, she'd be the star."

I chuckled. After seeing her in action, I found this easy to imagine. "Does Dee work outside the home?"

"No. For a while she lived in L.A. trying to make it as an actress, but when that dried up, she moved home and mooched off her parents until she and Aaron tied the knot." Lachlan raised a hand. "He's worked for me a few years, and I still can't figure out how the two of them ended up together."

"How so?" Laura asked.

"He came from nothing. She's got loads of family money. They must've had other things in common, but I never saw it." He squinted. "Guess she liked bad boys. You want to talk about upsetting the apple cart. Her parents were fit to be tied when she married Aaron. Rumor has it, they threatened to cut her out of their will."

Very interesting. "Did they?"

"No idea. Aaron never talked about his in-laws, but if he won them over, I wouldn't be surprised."

"Did Aaron and Dee seem happy?" I asked.

"Not lately. Aaron had been coming in late more often. Plus he was taking a lot of phone calls, and I could hear a woman screaming over the line." He shrugged. "Dee's pregnancy hormones?"

"Are you sure he was talking to Dee?" Hamlet asked.

"Can't say for certain," Lachlan said. "Might've been the mystery girl—or someone else."

I considered the rage Dee had shown toward Alexa. "Do you have any idea why Dee would've zeroed in on Alexa yesterday morning?"

"Aaron joked around with her like a kid sister. Maybe someone eating here witnessed it and got the wrong idea." He pressed his hands against the table and stood. "Hey, I've got work to do, so if there's nothing else . . ."

"No. Thanks for your help." As Lachlan went to greet some other customers, I swirled my Coke with the straw. "We have to figure out who that mystery girl is."

Laura leaned forward. "I'm not sure he's telling us the whole story. There *had* to be someone else who witnessed that incident with Aaron. It doesn't make sense that he and Aaron were the only ones working."

Alexa emerged from the kitchen with our hamburgers.

"How long have you worked here?" I asked.

She set the plate in front of me, and a rogue French fry slid onto the table. "Since January."

"Did you happen to be working one night this past winter when a girl who was really upset came to the back door looking for Aaron Lehman?" I popped a fry in my mouth.

"No." She set Laura's and Hamlet's plates down. "But wait a second . . . now that you mention it, the next day I heard about it from the chick who washed the dishes."

"Do you think she'd talk to us?" I asked.

"Probably, but she quit a while back to drive an ice cream truck. Her name's Clover Calloway."

CHAPTER TEN

After we finished our burgers, I checked social media and found Clover's Ice Cream was active on Instagram and Twitter—and that Clover and her truck were currently stationed at Lakeview Park.

Laura decided to give Hamlet and me some time alone, so we piled into his truck and drove to the park to find Clover. When we arrived, kids were shrieking and splashing in the lake while their parents watched from lawn chairs in the sand.

As Hamlet and I approached, I was thankful that Clover's truck was *not* playing the obnoxious, high-pitched music. "Do Your Ears Hang Low?" and "Pop Goes the Weasel" had been running on a loop in my head since Friday night.

Once again, Clover was sporting underwear-like denim shorts. This time, she'd added cowboy boots to her ensemble, and she wore a sleeveless kelly green polo. "You don't have your dog with you," she said.

"He's napping. I brought my boyfriend instead."

"Nice upgrade." She gave Hamlet the once over. "And her dog is gorgeous, so . . ." She batted her eyes.

I bristled. Miss Clover was about ten seconds from having one of her own ice cream bars jammed down her throat.

Nice Georgia. God really did have a lot of work to do on me.

Hamlet rested his hand on the small of my back. "I'd like a drumstick, please."

She turned to me. "For you?"

"Orange push-up." I held out a couple of bills. "My treat."

"Thanks, darling." He smiled at me.

Clover took my money and handed us our ice cream. "Can I ask you something, Georgia?"

Oh boy. "Sure." I ripped off the wrapper.

"I'll take that for you." She reached over, swiped the wrapper out of my hand, snatched Hamlet's trash, and tossed our garbage into a bin in her truck. "Are you a detective?"

I pushed up the orange sherbet. "I'm a farmer, but—"

"You're an amateur sleuth like Nancy Drew, right? Because when I was volunteering at the animal shelter, I overheard Sheila Thurston say her neighbor's friend and her pretty yellow dog were visiting and that she has an investigating hobby. I knew it had to be you."

I fought a snort. "I've helped solve a case or two. I wouldn't call it a hobby."

Or would I?

"She's being modest," Hamlet said. "She's solved more than a couple of cases." He winked.

Not helpful. I drilled him with a stare, but he grinned and resumed eating his ice cream.

"How'd you get started? I don't want to sell ice cream forever, and I might want to run a food truck, but I was also thinking I could become a private investigator. I should finish college, but I'm not into studying—or safe spaces."

I nearly choked. "I'm certainly not a private investigator—"

"Then how have you solved cases?"

"I chat with people, listen carefully, and pay attention to my surroundings." Since Hamlet was with me, I didn't mention that dating Cal had helped too.

"That's solid advice." She tapped her foot against the concrete. "Do you think the sheriff's department would let me go on a ride-along?"

"It wouldn't hurt to ask."

She leaned against the truck. "Speaking of listening carefully, nobody can stop talking about Aaron Lehman's murder. It's super scary. I hope we don't have a serial killer out there. What do you think?"

"It's more likely someone who knew Aaron killed him," I said. "Which is why I'd like to—"

"Here's my theory." She twisted her leather bracelet. "And since you're a detective, you can tell me if it's a good one. It'll be like you're mentoring me."

"Actually, I need to ask you about—"

"I think Aaron was selling drugs."

Hamlet and I exchanged glances. Had Aaron gone back to his old life?

She put a hand on her hip. "Now, I know we're not supposed to speak bad about dead people, but I know from working with Aaron at Lachlan's that he *definitely* struggled to make ends meet. His wife had grown up rich and never got over it."

I nearly choked—again.

"Do you have any proof he was dealing?" Hamlet asked.

Clover looked at me. "Remember how I told you I was invited to bring my truck to a party with a bunch of teenagers?"

"The ones who had a food fight?"

"Yep. Aaron was there and didn't even act like he knew me. Talked to a teenage girl for like two minutes and left. She had waist-length hair that needed a trim and a tattoo of the word *hope* right here." Clover tapped her right upper arm. "They both acted super shady, so I think Aaron was there to sell drugs. The party got way crazier after that. I had to leave because the kids were drinking—and smoking pot. I wasn't going to let those rich kids ruin my property—or get me in trouble."

"I don't blame you. Did you see Aaron and the girl exchange money?"

She reached for my empty push-up container before I could suck out every last bit of sweet nectar, and I had to fight the reflex to grab it.

"No," she said. "But they walked over by the parked cars, so they could've done a quick exchange. The whole thing seemed like a business transaction."

"Why do you say that?" Hamlet asked.

"Their body language. It wasn't romantic. They both looked super serious, and the girl skulked around like she was totally uncomfortable."

"You've been helpful." I withdrew a Winston Family Farms business card from my purse. "Give me a call if you see or hear anything else." I hoped I wouldn't regret giving her my phone number.

She shoved my card in her pocket. "Should I tell the detective who's investigating Aaron's murder what I witnessed at the party?"

"Yes. It wouldn't hurt to tell Detective McCloud. Now I have some questions for you." I forged ahead before she could interrupt. "When you worked with Aaron do you recall a crying girl coming to the back door at Lachlan's and asking for him on a snowy night?"

"Yeah. It was super dramatic, and I thought Lachlan was going to call the cops, but Aaron stepped in."

"Was it the same girl you saw Aaron talking to at the party?" I asked.

"No."

"Do you know who crying girl was?"

"I don't know her name, but I'd seen her at Hideaway Country Club. My first job was bussing tables there." She wrinkled her nose. "It wasn't fun watching a bunch of rich people look down their noses at me while I cleaned their dirty tables. I do know that chick has a lot of money, because she was carrying a Coach purse, and it wasn't a knock off. Her nails and hair were perfect—like she spends a ton at a salon."

"Did Aaron ever tell you what was wrong?"

"No, and I tried to get it out of him the next day, but all he'd say was that she was an old friend who needed help, and he didn't want to let her down." Clover lowered her voice. "Maybe she was into drugs and was looking for a fix."

"I hear you flip houses, Hamlet." Tommy wiped barbecue sauce off his hands, tossed his crumpled napkin aside, and grabbed a fresh one from the holder on the table.

That night, following an afternoon of swimming, we were on Laura's porch eating the wings Tommy had brought from a place in town.

"I've done some remodeling too." Hamlet turned to me. "Text Cal and have him send some pictures of his kitchen."

"Hold the phone." Tommy paused with a chicken wing in front of his mouth and looked back and forth between the two of us before his gaze landed on me. "Didn't you used to date a guy named Cal?"

"Yes." I ducked my head and sent the text, even though it felt seventeen kinds of awkward.

Tommy gaped at Hamlet. "Lemme see if I got this straight. You just told your girlfriend to text her *ex-boyfriend.*"

Hamlet tilted his head and studied Tommy with a measured

gaze. "Georgia and Cal are friendly neighbors. I'm not a fan of cellphones, so mine's in the car."

"Hmph." Tommy took a bite of his honey barbecue wing and chewed thoughtfully. "Not sure I'd do that." He licked his lips.

Hamlet helped himself to another round of coleslaw while I plunked my phone on the table. The unbalanced ceiling fan ticked an annoying rhythm, marking the conversational lull's passing seconds.

"Have you found another house to renovate?" Laura asked Hamlet.

He brightened. "I'm going to hold off on that a bit while I focus on my role in *The Music Man*. I sold my first flip, and I'm renting the apartment above Dan Filmore's garage."

The same apartment where Cal had once lived, which I tried not to let bother me every time I visited Hamlet.

But it did.

Laura wiped her fingers on a napkin. "I see."

Tick. Tick. Tick. Laura should have Hamlet take a look at that stupid fan.

She avoided my gaze, and there was no mistaking the disapproval in her tone. I didn't want to admit it, but her fears about Hamlet flaking on me might not be that far off. Before I launched into full freak-out mode, I needed to talk to him and find out where his head was.

After we finished supper, I asked Hamlet to walk with me to the beach. I needed to know my fears were unfounded, and I didn't need to panic about possibly giving up farming.

He took my hand, and we strolled in silence. A few kids played on the equipment in the common area. A breeze had blown away some of the oppressive humidity, making the evening more pleasant.

"I'm so glad Laura invited me," he said.

"I appreciate you taking time to be here." I cringed inwardly. That hadn't come out quite the way I intended.

Thankfully, my semi-snarky comment didn't appear to faze him. We arrived at the empty beach and sat on a bench facing the water. Waves lapped in and out against the seawall, and a gull swooped by.

"I *have* been neglecting our relationship as of late, and I apologize," he said.

"Thank you. I didn't want to make you feel like you can't pursue your dreams, and I'd never want to stand in your way. I just need to know where I fit into all of this and what you have in mind for the future—"

His lips met mine, and I let myself forget about everything else—for a few seconds.

He broke away. "Now, my darling, how can I set your mind at ease?"

Did he really think a kiss and telling me what I wanted to hear would solve everything? I was a bottom-line girl, and kissing him—while very nice—wasn't going to cut it when I needed answers. I should be more romantic, but that was a whole other issue.

"Are you going to pursue acting full time?" I blurted.

His face remained unchanged as he stroked my hair. "I haven't decided. I enjoy renovating, but I didn't think I'd miss being on stage as much as I have."

"Will you move back to Chicago—or somewhere else?"

"I don't know. *The Music Man* runs until the end of September. Perhaps I'll audition for the next production at Bell's." He gazed out at the water. "There are acting opportunities in Indianapolis."

But there weren't many. I twisted my amethyst ring. "Why not buy another house to flip? You have plenty of time before the end of September." I was practical to a fault, and from a business standpoint, his shillyshallying didn't make sense because acting wasn't exactly making him rich. It was all I could do not to haul off and tell him so.

Life Lesson #8: It's more important to be respectful than to be right.

He sighed. "I wish I could tell you there aren't any suitable properties, but you know that's not true. Honestly, my heart's not in flipping. I might take some odd jobs here and there or do another quick renovation."

"I want you to be happy, but where does this leave *us*? What if your next acting gig takes you halfway across the country?" I hadn't signed up for a long-distance relationship, and part of me couldn't help feeling duped.

"I'm willing to do whatever it takes to make things work. Are you saying you're not?"

"I don't know! How can I when I don't have a clue what that even means?" Why couldn't I be a woman who stuck her head in the sand and pretended everything was fine and that love would conquer all?

"Are you saying you're not willing to have a long-distance relationship?" he asked.

"No. I'm saying I can't follow you." I buried my face in my hands.

"Georgia Rae, that's never been my expectation," he said softly.

I lifted my head and met his sad, blue-gray eyes.

"But it would've meant the world to know you'd consider it."

CHAPTER ELEVEN

After my conversation with Hamlet, we walked back and endured another sunset cruise around the lake with Laura and Captain Tom-Tom. Hamlet and I managed to put on a good show, but my gut said Laura sensed the tension. I hoped she'd remember our truce and refrain from giving me her opinion on the matter. And considering Tommy's comments at dinner—I couldn't be sure our act convinced him either.

Since I wasn't in the mood for a movie when we returned, and Hamlet was going to bed, I went upstairs to my room and put on my leopard print jammie set. A few minutes later, my phone dinged. Cal had finally sent the pictures of his renovated kitchen.

My heart skittered—just a little—when I saw the design that looked exactly like what I would've chosen if I'd remodeled my own kitchen. White shaker cabinets. Quartz countertops. A tile backsplash. I'd certainly thought of renovating, because the 1980s style in my kitchen was getting tiresome. A girl could only claim flower-basket print wallpaper was nostalgic for so long. I typed out a quick response.

Looks great. Thanks for sending the pics.

I set my phone on the nightstand and threw back the comforter. My phone lit up, and I snatched it and read his response.

How are you?

I knew I should give him the short answer. A requisite—and very polite—*fine, thank you.* But when I thought of his blue eyes and handsome face—complete with a dimple, I couldn't quite get there. My fingers took on a life of their own.

I found a body in Lake Hideaway yesterday morning.

I sent the message, collapsed into the bed, and deleted emails. Seconds later, he called.

"Please tell me you're kidding," he said as soon as I answered.

Grinning, I pictured the look on Cal's face, but I quickly grew serious. "I wish. I bumped into the man after I fell while water skiing." I winced at the memory and gave Cal a quick recap.

"Merciful heavens," he muttered.

"Now you sound like me."

He chuckled, and I heard some keyboard clicks. "Found the article about it," he said.

"You didn't believe me?" I wasn't really offended, but I wanted to keep the conversation going.

Bad Georgia. Bad, bad Georgia.

"I definitely believed you. Just promise me you'll be careful."

"I'm on vacation."

"Uh-huh."

"From your tone, I assume you believe I'm poking around."

He laughed. "Aren't you?"

"Yes."

"Promise."

Even though we were technically still friends—and neighbors —it thrilled me that he cared. "I'll be careful." I couldn't resist asking one more question, because I'd been wondering about the matter for a couple of months, and I hadn't had a good opportunity. "How are Mason and Henry?"

Would Cal think I was being too nosy? He'd worked with Mason Thrailkill back when he'd been a detective in Cleveland, and Henry was Mason's two-year-old son.

"Getting by. Adjusting to life without Natalie hasn't been easy."

Several months earlier, Mason's wife had been murdered while riding her bike. Later, Mason received a letter that read, *How does it feel? You killed the person I loved. And now I've taken the one you love.* Police had zeroed in on two cases Mason had worked where the suspects died before evidence exonerated them.

Cal had been involved in one of the murder investigations, and fear of losing me the way Mason had lost Natalie had caused him to push me away—until we broke up.

"Have the police found her killer?" I asked.

"No. They can't seem to connect anyone from the cases he worked to Natalie's. Believe me. They've tried."

"I'll keep praying they'll find the missing link." That wasn't just something to say. I *had* been praying for this situation because I knew what it was like to live without answers when a loved one had been murdered.

"Thanks. I know Mason would appreciate it." A few seconds passed. "Well, I won't keep you," he said quickly. "Take care."

"You too." I set my phone on the nightstand with a sigh, clicked off the lamp, and prayed I'd be able to sleep.

Arlene's Café and Variety Store was located north of Lake Hide-away deep in Amish country. The next morning, while Hamlet drove us there in his truck, I brought him up to speed on everything Byron and Minnie Collins had told us about Aaron the night we'd watched fireworks.

A sign for the store and cafe pointed down a rural road lined with soybean fields, so he turned off the highway and dodged a few road apples. Plain white houses with large gardens gracing the yards dotted the countryside. Horse barns and fences were scattered over the landscape. The store stood across the road from a house and a barn, and Hamlet entered the gravel lot and parked next to the building. To my right, a horse and buggy waited at the hitching post. The chestnut horse flicked his tail as if he were impatient.

The porch held several unfinished rocking chairs with dangling price tags, and Byron sat in one. He stowed his sunglasses in his shirt pocket and stood slowly as we approached. "There's my favorite heroine." Byron rested his hand on his back as if it ached, and his arm was bandaged. "Thanks for fishing my wife and me out of the water yesterday."

"Glad I could help." We made introductions and settled in the rocking chairs. "How are you feeling?" I tucked my hair behind my ear as a gust caused the wind chimes to jingle.

"Beaten up, but lucky." He patted his cheek that was also covered. "A plastic surgeon stitched up my face and said I shouldn't have too bad a scar. I'm disappointed. So much for my dream of looking like a pirate." He rocked back and forth. "Arrghh!"

At least he had a good attitude. "What do you think caused the explosion?"

"Probably just built-up fumes igniting, but we'll know soon. I should've run the blower, but neither one of us smelled fumes. But that might not mean anything because Minnie has allergies, and I've got a terrible sense of smell." He shook his head. "We got in a hurry to beat the brunch rush. It could've been a lot worse. God was looking out for us."

There was another possibility I had to ask about, given everything I'd learned about the town's marinas. "How long ago did you have your boat serviced?"

"Saturday—over at Sutcliffe Marina." The color drained from Byron's face. "You don't think . . .?"

"If there was a leak in the boat's fuel line, it wouldn't matter how long you ran the blower—if fuel accumulated in the bilge and a spark hit it," I said.

"They knew I had trouble getting my boat to start sometimes . . . no. I can't think that way." He leaned forward. "Don Sutcliffe would be furious if he knew I was speculating his marina might be responsible for my boat blowing up. Still . . . I've heard rumors about the service department cutting corners ever since Craig took over."

"What else have you heard?" Hamlet asked as he glanced at me.

"Please," Byron said. "Drop it. We have no reason to believe that the accident was anything but my own stupid fault."

Interesting that he was so eager to protect the Sutcliffes. "Okay." I made a lip-zipping motion. The sound of horse hooves clip-clopping against the road grew louder.

A buggy turned into the parking lot, and after securing his horse, a young Amish man with a sandy beard lining his jaw joined us on the porch. Byron introduced him as Moses Zook.

As we entered the café, the aroma of fresh-baked bread welcomed us. To our left was a seating area with oak tables and chairs, and the walls were painted a country blue, with a floral border lining the ceiling. A glass case held cookies, pies, and breads, and a shelf was laden with apple butter, jams, and bags of homemade noodles. A young Amish girl in a lavender-colored dress worked behind the counter. Two Amish men sat at a table next to a lace-curtained window and appeared to be finishing cinnamon rolls.

On the right were aisles of bulk goods like nuts and candies as well as groceries. There were work shoes, sewing notions, and canning supplies. The store certainly lived up to the variety in its name.

Byron led the way to a round table in the corner, and once we were seated, he pointed at the menu printed on the scalloped placemat. "If you'd like a recommendation, Arlene is known for her biscuits and gravy, which is my favorite." Byron looked at Hamlet, Moses, and me. "But you can't go wrong with anything on the menu."

"Biscuits and gravy are perfect for me," Hamlet flipped over his coffee mug. "And a cinnamon roll. Georgia tells me they're legendary."

"I'll have the same," Moses added.

I should probably pass on such a rich breakfast, because unlike my slim boyfriend, I had a few more curves than I liked— though I didn't work very hard to remedy that situation. But when the young Amish girl that Moses introduced as his cousin Lizzie Zook filled our coffee cups and took our orders, I went along with everyone else.

Biscuit-and-gravy peer pressure.

I curled my fingers around my coffee mug. "Moses, thanks for taking the time to meet with us."

He nodded slightly. "I'll do what I can to help—but I'm not sure I know much."

"You may know more than you realize," Byron said.

"Byron mentioned that Aaron was considering becoming Amish," I said. "What can you tell us about that?"

96

Moses stroked his beard. "It sounds odd, Aaron wanting to convert, but it wasn't. Aaron's dad grew up Amish and left as a teenager. In a way, it was like Aaron was getting back to his roots."

"Do you think that's why he was drawn to you when you worked at the RV factory together?" I asked.

"No. We already knew each other." Moses smiled sadly. "We're first cousins."

CHAPTER TWELVE

I mulled over Moses's statement. This place wasn't any different than my hometown, where everybody was related to everyone else. In fact, I'd made good and sure Hamlet and I weren't long-lost cousins before we'd started dating. Even Cal had relatives in Wildcat Springs, though he'd grown up in Ohio.

I pushed the intrusive thought about my ex-boyfriend aside. "I see." I glanced at Byron and Hamlet, who seemed to be enjoying witnessing this conversation.

"I had no idea," Byron said.

"My mom and his dad are—were—sister and brother," Moses said. "They've both passed on."

I folded the edge of my placemat as another cousin connection came to mind. "Are you related to Rachel Thurston?"

"That's my sister. She chose not to be baptized and left us when she was eighteen. She comes around once a year or so, though she's welcome in my home any time."

Funny how Sheila had never mentioned her daughter-in-love's Amish background.

Moses cleared his throat. "After Aaron started working at the factory, he told me he was thinking about joining our church. I discussed the matter with my wife Ellen, and she suggested we invite him to stay in our *dawdi haus* for a trial run. My parents had passed, and the house was sitting empty."

I sipped my coffee. "How long did Aaron stay?"

"Two weeks. I think he'd decided after the first few days that our way wasn't for him, but I reckon he viewed it as a vacation and enjoyed the change of pace."

"From his wife?" I asked.

"No," Moses said. "Aaron and Dee hadn't married yet, and she wasn't very happy about him possibly becoming Amish. However, he decided to marry her during his retreat. After he left, he proposed, and they married. Then he quit the factory to go to college and work at that restaurant in Hidden Shores."

I unwrapped my silverware from the napkin and set it on the paper placemat. "Were Dee and Aaron happy?"

Moses shifted, folded his hands, and rested them on the table. "People have different expectations of what happiness means." He couldn't quite meet my eyes. "I'm sorry I can't tell you more."

Can't or won't? Hamlet nudged my foot under the table, but I didn't even have to try to keep the question from popping out because Lizzie brought our plates of biscuits and gravy.

Hamlet offered to bless the food, and when he'd finished, I had more I needed to ask Moses before I could fully enjoy my breakfast. "Moses, did Aaron ever talk about his brother-in-law, Craig Sutcliffe?"

Moses cut a piece of biscuit with the edge of his fork. "He mentioned once that he thought Craig was a bully, but he never went into detail."

Byron set his fork on his plate. "I can't speak for Craig's relationship with Aaron, but I've witnessed Craig speak disrespectfully to his parents on more than one occasion. Though, that certainly doesn't mean he killed Aaron."

Byron's assertion served to bolster my opinion of Craig's character, but Byron was right. Having a nasty temper and being disrespectful didn't necessarily make Craig a killer. "Did Aaron ever say anything about plans to work at Sutcliffe Marina when he finished college?"

Moses nodded. "His father-in-law was trying to talk him into it, but Aaron wasn't so sure he wanted to be involved in the family business. He wanted to make his own way."

I had a feeling that wasn't Aaron's only reason, but I was certain Moses wouldn't say. "I'm almost done with the questions, and then you can eat in peace."

"I don't mind," Moses said.

"Hamlet and I spoke to a witness who saw Aaron at a party with a bunch of teenagers in Hidden Shores—and this person indicated that he might've been there to sell drugs. Do you have any reason to believe that he'd gone back to that life?"

Seconds ticked by as Moses appeared to ponder my question, but when he spoke, he looked me straight in the eyes. "When Aaron died, I hadn't seen him for a month or so. But if I had to guess, I'd say no. He was too focused on work, getting his college degree, and the new baby. I don't think he'd risk everything he'd earned by going to prison again."

This made sense, and Clover *had* been speculating—or maybe even lying—about what she'd witnessed. I considered a different angle. "Did Aaron know any other kids who've chosen to leave the Amish community and might've been at the party?"

Surprise flickered in Moses's expression. "I certainly can't think of anyone."

If that was true, and I sensed Moses believed he was speaking honestly, then why had Aaron been at that wild party?

After Byron and Moses left, Hamlet and I browsed through the store, and I decided to buy a package of pecan cinnamon rolls to share with Laura. I picked up a foil container and approached the counter while Hamlet continued perusing the variety store aisles.

"These rolls are so great, I had to take some back to my friend," I said to our waitress Lizzie.

"I'm glad," she said. "I'll be sure to tell Arlene."

I held out the money, but as she took my coins, she dropped one. When she lunged to catch it, her short dress sleeve inched upward, revealing the word *hope* tattooed in cursive on her right, upper arm.

No. Way. An Amish girl with a tattoo? *Be cool, Georgia.* It was too late, because my eyes had already bugged.

Could Lizzie be the girl Clover had seen talking to Aaron at the party? Lizzie's *kapp* hid her hair, but it was probably long. Her simple upbringing might've made her appear uncomfortable at a shindig with a bunch of wild teenagers.

Lizzie followed my gaze, yanked on her sleeve, and tossed the rolls in a plastic bag. "Have a nice day." She thrust the sack toward me.

"Did you talk to Aaron Lehman at a party in Hidden Shores last weekend?" I blurted.

"No." She blanched. "Aaron's my cousin, and I'm sorry he passed away, but you have me confused with someone else. Excuse me. I hear the oven timer buzzing." She darted into the back room.

But I didn't hear a thing.

"It's not surprising Lizzie didn't want to speak to you about seeing Aaron at the party," Hamlet said as he drove us back to

Laura's house. "She probably doesn't want anyone overhearing what she's been doing during her *rumspringa*."

"I agree." That was the period of freedom Amish kids had before becoming baptized and committing to the plain lifestyle. "Clover must've misinterpreted what she saw. Since Aaron and Lizzie were cousins, maybe he heard she was taking up with some rough kids and was there to warn her."

"He'd want to look after a family member, knowing how badly drugs can mess up a person's life."

We crested a hill, and the north edge of Little Hideaway came into view. Trees enclosed most of the tiny lake, but the tranquil water peeking through glistened. A few cabins were tucked into the hills. Hamlet veered onto Lake Loop Road.

"Did you get the feeling Moses Zook was holding back?" I asked.

"Yes." He tapped his thumb against the steering wheel. "You're fortunate he was willing to meet with us at all. I suspect he knows more about Aaron and Dee's problems than he was willing to share with strangers."

Fleetwood Mac's "Go Your Own Way" came on the radio, and he turned up the volume and sang along in his gorgeous baritone. He loved classic rock, but was he trying to give me a hint about our relationship? Or was he oblivious? I decided he was clueless when "Hey Jude" played next, and he continued to sing as we rounded Lake Hideaway.

He turned into Laura's subdivision, and in spite of last night's tension and my persistent uncertainty about our relationship's future, I wasn't ready for him to leave. He parked in her driveway, and we got out and lingered next to his truck.

"Darling, I need to get on the road." Hamlet took my hand and put it up to his heart. "Promise me you'll be careful."

I couldn't help thinking of Cal making the same request. "I promise." I met Hamlet's gaze. "One more thing."

"Yes?"

"I'm sorry about last night. Your career change is just taking me by surprise. I need to wrap my head around what it means —for us."

He hugged me. "I understand. I haven't made any final decisions."

My heart skittered. "I'm looking forward to seeing you play Professor Hill. You know, I always thought playing Marian the Librarian would be a blast, even though I don't read all that much, and did you know that I played Amaryllis when I was a middle school and—"

He always knew the right moment to silence my babbling with a kiss.

We broke apart.

"Enjoy the rest of your vacation, Georgia Rae." He got in his truck, cranked the engine, and opened the window.

"I will." I meant it—and I certainly appreciated that he understood my need to find justice and didn't try to stop me.

He blew a kiss, and I stood waving as he drove off.

"Have you solved the case yet?"

I jumped.

Behind me, Sheila had materialized in Laura's driveway. *Merciful heavens.* It was like she teleported from place to place.

"No," I said.

"Well, what've you found out?"

I played a mental game of tug-of-war. How much could I trust Sheila? But if I didn't keep her in the loop, I might lose her as a source—or she might even use her influence to keep others in town from talking to me. But. The way she was always skulking around eavesdropping didn't sit well with me, which made me a hypocrite since I'd made good and sure to eavesdrop on Dee when she confronted Alexa at Lachlan's Lighthouse. Not to mention, Sheila was always running down her daughter-in-law, and I'd yet to come across any evidence to suggest Rachel had been having an affair.

At least at home I had the advantage of knowing people's reputations. Right now, all I had was my gut instincts, and giving Sheila a tidbit might help in the long run. "This morning Hamlet and I met your daughter-in-law's brother, Moses."

"Good work. I wondered how long it'd take you to uncover Rachel's Amish past. He have anything important to say?"

"We'd suspected that Aaron may've been selling drugs again, but after speaking with Moses, I don't think that's the case."

"Who told you Aaron was into drugs?"

"Clover, the ice cream girl, saw Aaron at a party and suspected he was selling."

Sheila snorted. "I wouldn't believe a thing that gossiping money grubber says. I'm glad Moses set you straight. When was this so-called party?"

"Last weekend."

"Hmph. I don't think so." Sheila removed her phone from her back pocket, scrolled, and turned the phone so I could see a picture from Dee Sutcliffe's Instagram account. "Aaron and Dee went on a babymoon to Chicago last weekend."

Laura was the proud owner of a brand-new WaveRunner, and she'd given me permission to take it out while she was at work. Since the afternoon had turned even steamier than the morning, I decided it was the perfect time for a ride around the lake to think through everything I'd learned so far.

I buckled my life jacket, slid the key fob over my wrist, and went outside. After securing my phone and wallet in the waterproof compartment, I spun the lift's wheel and eased the watercraft into the channel.

I slipped onto the seat and got the engine to purr without a battle. My grandpa had owned an older model that'd always taken a good deal of coaxing to start. As I idled down the channel, I spotted some turtles sunning themselves on a log, and as I glugged by, they dove for cover.

When I passed the buoy line, I zoomed north. Since it was a weekday afternoon, only a few boats were scattered around. Squeezing the throttle, I giggled as my hair blew back and water misted my face.

I entered Calloway Cove, performed a few three-sixties, and managed to avoid dumping myself into the secluded inlet's choppy water. The public piers on the Calloway Cove side of Lakeview Park were empty, but trees blocked my view of the swimming area overlooking Smith Bay. I buzzed around the peninsula, where I could see the beach action.

Clover had parked her ice cream truck in the lot. It wouldn't hurt to stop and ask her a few follow-up questions about the party where she'd theorized Aaron was selling drugs, especially since Lizzie Zook matched Clover's description. Maybe she had her parties or dates confused, or Sheila was right, and Clover wasn't reliable.

I zipped back around the peninsula, floated to the public pier, and tied the WaveRunner to a metal post. After retrieving my phone and wallet, I hurried through the trees to the beach. There were no signs of life around the ice cream truck, which seemed weird since there were plenty of kids digging in the sand and splashing in the water. When I drew closer to Clover's truck, I read a handwritten sign tucked under the windshield wipers.

Be back soon. Clover

I surveyed the cement block building near the parking lot. Maybe she'd gone to the restroom. There wasn't much else around.

Pushing a stroller, a thin young woman in yoga pants stalked past me, stopped, and turned around. "I wouldn't wait if I were you." She scowled. "My kid's been asking for a fudge bar for an hour." She pointed at a little boy who looked about three. He grasped a half-eaten animal cracker and smiled at me as if he weren't too heartbroken over missing out on ice cream.

I glanced back at the truck. Clover would had to have walked or taken a boat to wherever she'd gone, because Hidden Shores was located on the opposite end of the lake. "Did you see Clover leave?"

"Yep. She hopped in a turquoise VW bus—right as we were heading over." Her eyes flashed. "This is no way to run a business."

Life Lesson #938: Never deny a stressed-out momma her fudgy bar.

"I'm sure Clover has a good excuse. Did you recognize the person who picked her up?"

"No." She scoffed and looked at me as if I'd lost my mind before storming to the parking lot.

I headed for the beach and asked a few people if they knew who the ice cream girl had left with. No luck. Unless I counted the strange and slightly irritated looks I got.

I lounged on a park bench for another ten minutes or so before the afternoon sun started to fry my fair skin. It was time to get back on the WaveRunner and get some air flowing, so I hurried through the trees to the piers. I could always track Clover down later—or send her a message via social media.

I puttered out of Calloway Cove, and as I headed toward the middle of the lake, an engine revved. A large personal watercraft rocketed toward me, though the driver had thousands of acres to give me a wide berth.

I screeched, squeezed the throttle, and blasted south toward Laura's channel. I glanced over my shoulder.

The watercraft must've been a racing model because it was

easily gaining on me. The driver wore a blue, long-sleeved T-shirt, bulky black life jacket, and a helmet.

I banked left, but the driver followed. I jerked the Wave-Runner right, to make sure I wasn't being paranoid.

I wasn't.

CHAPTER THIRTEEN

Lord, help!

Leaning forward, I barreled onward at wide-open speed. Water sprayed my face, and my hair whooshed backward. My thudding heart missed a beat, and I whipped my head back and forth, in search of a boat from the sheriff's department.

Nothing.

I peeked over my shoulder as Crazy Driver sped closer. The watercraft was all black—except for a red, orange, and yellow flame decal emblazoned on the front.

The driver zoomed within two feet of me.

Before I could react, my hunter revved the engine and veered around me, dousing me with water. The wake tipped me as I swerved. I let up on the throttle, lost my balance, and tumbled into the lake.

I surfaced, brushing hair from my eyes and snorting water from my nose. I spun around. Crazy Driver was long gone.

Laura's WaveRunner was floating away, so I swam after it.

"Ma'am, are you okay?" a teenage girl in a mint-green bikini yelled from a water trampoline. A teenage boy in yellow hibiscus-print trunks stood next to her while a few little kids swam around the trampoline.

"A little stunned." I caught hold of the watercraft.

"That was like a movie," the teenage boy said.

The girl shot a withering glare at him.

I hauled my shaking body on board—and thankfully it only took one try. "Whatever that person was driving sure had a lot of power." I slid forward on the seat and drew a ragged breath to slow my racing heart.

"It was a BlackBlaze 8200 performance model—for racing," the boy said. "That's why the dude had on a helmet."

My mind churned. I'd never heard of that model. "Are they very common?"

"Not the 8200s. At least, *I've* never seen one on this lake. BlackBlaze is a fairly new company." He shaded his eyes and looked out at the water.

"I haven't either, and I'm out here almost every weekday babysitting." The girl motioned toward the kids.

"Maybe the guy just got it," the boy said. "I'm so jealous."

"How do you know it was a guy?" The girl blinked at him with annoyance. "The driver could've been a woman."

He snorted. "Whatever."

I attempted to rein in my scattered thoughts. "Who sells them?"

He turned to me. "Thurston's Marina is the only authorized dealer on the lake."

A good friend would never run gas out of a WaveRunner without replacing it, so before I returned to Laura's house, I took a detour to Thurston's Marina. On the way there, I drove by Lakeview Park to search for trailers small enough to haul any brand of personal watercraft, but there were only two empty boat trailers attached to trucks.

Either Crazy Driver lived on the lake or rented a pier space.

I slowed as I approached Thurston's. A newly constructed metal building had replaced the musty old wooden structure I remembered. An imposing brick sign and beautifully landscaped exterior contrasted with Sutcliffe Marina's weedy bushes and dilapidated facade.

While the attendant was filling the tank, I wandered inside to the showroom. Large windows let in sunlight, and different models of speedboats were positioned around the spacious room. I made a beeline for the BlackBlaze 8200 model. The massive personal watercraft boasted a seat big enough for three people.

Keith Thurston emerged from his office. "Hey there, Georgia. You looking to buy?" He appeared more energetic than the last couple of times I'd seen him.

I hitched my thumb toward the BlackBlaze. "That's a beauty. I bet it's fun to ride."

"Lot of power," he said. "I wouldn't recommend a racing model. The 6200 is enough power for a recreational boater." He pointed to a red model to his left. "But if you like speed, I'm happy to fix you up."

I ran my hand over the 8200's flame decal. "Do you sell very many racing models?"

"No. But a lot of young guys like looking at 'em."

"If you had to guess, how many racing models are on Lake Hideaway?"

"Not sure," he said. "Probably three or four. Why?"

"Someone tried to run me down with one this afternoon, and I'm interpreting it as a warning."

"Why would . . .? Oh." He glanced over his shoulder and whispered, "Because Mom asked you to nose around in Aaron's case?"

"Right."

"She shouldn't have done that. I'm not a suspect."

"She meant well," I said.

"Come into my office for a minute." He led the way to the room with a view of the show floor. A framed black-and-white photo of an antique wood boat hung on the wall behind his desk. He closed the door and motioned to the upholstered chair in front of the desk.

I glanced at the damp shorts I was wearing over my bathing suit.

"Relax," Keith said. "A little lake water won't hurt the chair."

I perched on the edge and moved my wet braid around so it wouldn't drip onto the fabric. The chill from the air conditioning caused goosebumps to pepper my arms.

"I probably shouldn't do this, but I'm going to let you see a list of people on Hideaway who've purchased the 8200's since we began selling them a couple of years ago." He sat and typed. "Aaron meant a lot to my wife, and I want to see justice served."

I had more questions for Keith, but my gut told me to hold off on a couple until I had the list in hand. So, I started with the most benign inquiry. "Speaking of the case, did Aaron ever mention helping a friend in need this past winter? She's young, petite with nice hair and nails. Carries a Coach purse. She's been seen at the country club." Although, if Clover had given me bad information, this description wouldn't be helpful.

"Not to me. If Rachel were around, I'd tell you to talk to her since she and Aaron were tight, but she's off taking a break from being my wife—and Julian's mother. Still, if I had to guess, your description sounds like Aaron's ex-girlfriend Valerie Hudson. She's loaded, so she probably spent time at the country club."

"Does she live in Hidden Shores?"

"I don't know, but I bet my mom would be happy to tell you." He angled the monitor toward me. "See any familiar names?"

I ran my finger down the list of people on the screen. Jason Singer, John Hill, Danielle DuPont, and Buck Templeton. I didn't recognize a single name. I held up my phone. "Mind if I take a picture?"

"Go for it."

I snapped a photo. "Thanks." I wasn't sure if this information would be helpful, but I had to try.

"No problem." He turned the monitor.

"I'm curious about something else."

He leaned back and propped his ankle on his knee. "Ask away."

"When your mom recruited me to help, she mentioned you were warning your customers about problems with boats that'd been serviced at Sutcliffe Marina. What kind of issues were you seeing?"

"You name it," he said. "Years ago, I worked for my dad as a mechanic, so I know my stuff. I had a guy come in here this spring with a crack in the engine block because some idiot at Sutcliffe hadn't drained all the water while they were winterizing the boat. The water froze and caused the damage."

"Wow. What else?"

"I've heard people complain about mistakes on invoices. Repair estimates being way off." He shook his head. "The worst happened a couple of months ago. They forgot to put the drain plug in some poor woman's boat. It almost sank the first time she took it out. Those are the incidents I know about. Who knows what else they've messed up or how many lawsuits they're dealing with?"

Draining water during winterizing and putting in a drain plug were rookie mistakes. "So it's plausible that they could've missed a leaky fuel line when a boat was in for service?"

He studied me. "Are you talking about Mayor Collins's boat?"

"Yes."

"It wouldn't surprise me. I heard the mayor had his boat serviced at Sutcliffe Marina on Saturday." He shifted. "Look, a while back I reached out to Craig Sutcliffe and let him know about the damage I was seeing. I didn't want any customers to get hurt or to lose their hard-earned money. But nothing changed, so I had no choice but to warn people. I wasn't trying to put them out of business. They were doing that to themselves."

"Why didn't you talk to Don Sutcliffe?"

"I tried. He wouldn't take my calls."

"Why?"

"Don despises our family because my dad gave Don a run for his money when he made improvements to this place. I inherited the hatred along with our business when my dad passed. Besides, Don isn't involved in the day-to-day operations. Craig runs the marina, and he hates me even more than his dad."

"Had you heard Don wanted to replace Craig with Aaron?"

"Yeah. I figured it was a rumor because Aaron would've had to win over his father-in-law first, but maybe he did. He was a persuasive guy. I do know the idea for Aaron to meet with me was Craig's." Keith picked up his phone from his desk, swiped it, and scooted it toward me. "Check out this text from Aaron."

Craig Sutcliffe asked me to meet with you about the marina problem.

"Interesting."

"I think Craig was finally so desperate to save their marina that he was going to have Aaron bribe me to keep my mouth shut if lawyers came sniffing around," he said.

"What makes you say that?"

"Keep reading." He pointed at the phone.

I skimmed through the remaining thread, in which Keith had

claimed he was trying to keep people safe and Aaron had insisted on resolving the matter in person. They'd also arranged a meeting time. Then, I read the final message from Aaron.

> Thanks, man. I promise this meeting will be worth more than just your time.

———

When I returned to Laura's house, Sheila barged outside before I even had the WaveRunner docked on the lift. "You have any new leads on who killed Aaron?"

I hopped off and spun the lift's wheel. "Not really." It wasn't necessary to inform Sheila that after talking to her son, I'd be looking even more closely at Craig Sutcliffe, but I wasn't sorry she'd come over to talk to me. "What do you know about Aaron's ex-girlfriend Valerie Hudson?" I followed Sheila into her yard.

"That's a blast from the past." Sheila blinked and sat at her picnic bench. "What do you want to know?" She patted the table. "Have a seat."

I slipped onto the seat across from her. "I'd like to talk to her about Aaron."

"She couldn't have killed him, if that's what you're thinking." She crumbled a dried leaf between her fingers and brushed the pieces from the table.

"Why not?"

"Valerie grew up in my church, and I've known her parents since they were teenagers in our youth group. She's a beautiful girl."

Clearly, we were going around the barn to get to the horse, but her wandering thoughts gave me a chance to get some clarification about Valerie. "Petite? Likes to go to the salon? Into Coach purses?"

"That's her. Her mama bought her a Coach purse when she was a teenager. Why a teenager needs an expensive handbag is beyond me." She stood, opened a storage shed, removed a broom, and swept the pavement. "Valerie has a beautiful singing voice, but she dated Aaron during his wild years and got into drugs. It was a real shame to see her go down that road. After he went to prison, I heard she got clean. Not long ago, she relapsed and is back in rehab in a long-term program in Texas."

"How long is the program?"

"A year. I heard she's been gone since last winter, which is why she didn't kill Aaron."

Last winter.

If she was the mystery girl who'd showed up at Lachlan's, then her drug problem could be why she'd turned to Aaron for help. I probably couldn't even contact her if I knew where she was, but Detective McCloud could. Then I had another idea. "Do you think her family might talk to me?"

"She's an only child, and her parents died in a car accident last year. None of her other family lives around here." Sheila finished sweeping and put her broom away. "If I had to guess, I'd say losing her family caused her to relapse."

With Gus at my feet, I stood in front of the whiteboard in Laura's office where I'd added Valerie Hudson's name and the list of the BlackBlaze 8200 owners Keith had given me. After researching the owners on social media, I couldn't find any connections to Aaron Lehman or anyone in the Sutcliffe family, so giant question marks remained next to the names.

I picked up Laura's Lake Hideaway directory on her coffee table and searched for the names of lake property owners, which were listed in order by pier numbers. Though I found three of the

BlackBlaze owners in the book, none of them lived near Craig, and one owner, Danielle DuPont, wasn't listed at all. Aaron and Dee hadn't lived on the lake.

Slapping the book shut, I decided to call Detective McCloud so he could follow up. After he answered, I explained what'd happened, what I'd found, and how I'd hit a dead end in my research.

"Send me the picture with the names." He sighed. "Now, I know you want to help and are good at finding information, but someone sent you a clear warning to back off. I strongly suggest you don't go putting yourself in more danger."

"You're right." Goosebumps rose on my arms, and I wished Hamlet had been able to stay longer. Or that I was back home and Cal—no. I wasn't going there. "I'll focus on enjoying my vacation, but . . . if I see or hear anything strange, I'll let you know."

"Fair enough," Detective McCloud said. "Be sure to watch your back."

CHAPTER FOURTEEN

When I'd promised Detective McCloud that I'd focus on enjoying my vacation, golf had not been a part of that plan, because this girl didn't waste her time chasing a tiny ball around a pasture. I'd much rather take another sunset cruise around the lake or play a round of Mexican train dominoes.

However, Laura and Tommy had a different idea as to how we'd spend the evening, so to appease my hostess, I donned khaki capris and a teal polo and agreed to play one of the most ridiculous games known to man.

Attempt to play might be a more accurate way to describe the situation. At the very least, it would help me get my mind off Crazy Driver. Since I'd already told Detective McCloud, I decided not to worry Laura and kept the incident to myself.

Hideaway Country Club was a stately, red brick building on the lake's eastern shore. The golf course was located in the rolling hills across Lake Loop Road. Tommy had picked a great time for us to play because the parking lot was about half full, and thankfully, when we arrived at the first tee, no one was there to witness my impending humiliation.

"It's your lucky day." Tommy stopped in the shade of a huge sycamore and hopped out of the cart he was sharing with Laura.

"How so?" I sat frozen, gripping the steering wheel at ten and two.

He walked around my cart, removed a club from my borrowed bag, and held it out. "Not only do you get a complimentary lesson with a professional"—he tapped his chest—"you get to try out these awesome Grand Gertie clubs free of charge."

I got out and took the club with a massive head. "Hashtag blessed." I tried to sound grateful but landed around mildly sarcastic.

"Don't worry. I'm still learning." Laura gazed at Tommy. "But he's the best teacher, and the scramble format is fun when you're learning."

"Thanks, baby doll." He kissed her forehead and faced me. "Now, the way this is gonna work is I'll hit a shot. We'll go to those red tees up there." He pointed about a hundred yards away. "You and Laura will hit. Then we take the best shot of the three."

"Which will be yours," I said.

"Maybe. I've been known to slice and send my ball into the woods. Nobody hits great shots all the time." He patted my shoulder. "Golf isn't a game of perfect."

There's Life Lesson #24,222. "You never know. I might have a hidden talent." I flexed an arm muscle. "But don't hold your breath."

"I've been known to come through with a shot that we use— once or twice," Laura said. "I'm more help around the green."

"After we all hit our drives, we'll put the balls where the best shot landed and hit again." Tommy removed a club from his bag and took a few practice swings.

"And the purpose of this is?" I really was trying to sound nice, but my effort wasn't up to par. I fought a snort over my dorky pun.

"You don't have to feel bad about your score." He winked. "Besides, I'll give you plenty of pointers."

Tommy to the rescue. All was right with the world.

At least I'd be able to handle the putting. I had won some rounds of miniature golf when Brandi, Ashley, and I had played. I hoped they were having a nice time on their vacations. I'd have to send Ashley a selfie of me on the golf course, because she'd think it was hilarious. She'd stopped trying to get me to play a long time ago.

"Now, Georgia. The green is straight ahead. See the flag?" He pointed at the blue flag waving in the distance.

"Yep." I was golf inept. Not blind.

"This is a par four, so we want to get the ball into the hole in four shots. If you aim at the center of the fairway—the short grass in the middle—you'll be in good shape. Try to stay out of the bunker." He pointed at the white sand beckoning on the left.

"Tommy, she knows that much." Laura shot me a look that clearly said, *right?*

I manufactured a smile. "Four shots. Stay in the short grass, and don't visit the beach." I gave him a thumbs up.

Tommy sauntered over to the tee, performed some sort of preshot booty jig, swung, and sent the ball soaring onto the fairway. He had to have whacked it nearly three hundred yards.

I applauded. "If this is a team effort, then why do Laura and I even need to hit when you've already put the ball by the green?"

"Practice." He dropped the club into his bag. "Let's go." He jumped in the cart, and we drove to the red tees and stopped. "Laura, go ahead."

She hopped out—in her darling blue plaid golf skirt—and hit a respectable shot into the center of the fairway. As I'd suspected, she didn't hit nearly as far as Tommy, even with the advantage of over one hundred yards.

I tugged on the old golf glove I'd borrowed from Laura.

Clutching the enormous club Tommy had handed me, I approached the tee area, placed the ball on the tee, and tried to set up my stance to look like Laura's. No one needed to see me perform a booty jig like Tommy's.

"Bend at the waist a little more." Tommy and his gold chain ambled over and faced me.

I obeyed and adjusted my grip on the club.

"Now, the biggest mistake people make is they try to kill the ball. Bring the club back nice and easy. Keep your eye on the ball. Don't let your head pop up. Follow through."

The ball is Tommy.

Tommy is the ball.

I kept my eye on the little white enemy. I was going to win. I drew back and rotated my hips. Didn't I remember Ashley talking about how a golfer should always turn—never sway?

I followed through and hit the ball with a thwack. Keeping my head down, I staggered backward, and when I regained my balance, I shielded my eyes and looked up. "Where'd it go?"

"Nice shot!" Laura yelled.

"Holy cannoli! She's been holding out on us!" Tommy's jaw dropped. "You've really never played?" He turned to Laura. "I thought you said she didn't have any athletic ability. She drilled that thing. She's got one of the best natural swings I've seen in a long time, and I've seen a lot of swings."

"The unathletic one is standing right here! Where's my ball?"

Tommy pointed. "Sweetheart, it landed in front of the green —about ten yards away from mine."

Whoa. I put the club back in the bag. "It has to be beginner's luck."

"Maybe. But whatever you're doing, keep it up." Shaking his head, he climbed back in the cart and drove down the paved path.

I smirked as I followed them. No problem. I could definitely keep pretending the ball was Tommy.

I truly wish I could say that my streak of drilling shots straight down the fairway continued, and I left Tommy speechless time and time again, but that didn't happen. However, my golf aptitude wasn't nearly as bad as I'd imagined, and I'd managed to contribute more than putts.

Still, by the time we reached the green on the eighth hole, I was ready to be done and hadn't changed my mind about the game being a pointless waste of time. And in spite of my vow to stop investigating, I hadn't been able to keep my mind off the case.

Tommy bent and surveyed the green while Laura stood over her pink golf ball. "Aim at the left edge of the cup, baby doll."

Laura putted, and the ball raced a good thirty feet across the green and died in the cup.

She shrieked, which led to Tommy picking her up, swirling her around, and kissing her so enthusiastically that I had to look away.

Before I could vomit in my mouth, I went with the old subject-change trick as we walked off the green. "I have a question for you, Tommy."

"Shoot."

"Do you happen to know Valerie Hudson?"

He slipped his putter into his golf bag. "Name sounds familiar, but I can't place her."

"Who is she?" Laura pocketed her golf ball.

"Aaron Lehman's ex-girlfriend." I decided to be vague about the day's investigative activities. "Sheila told me Valerie went to drug rehab about six months ago."

"You think Valerie is the mystery girl Clover saw at Lachlan's?" Laura got into the cart.

"Exactly." I followed Tommy and Laura to the ninth—and mercifully—last hole.

As we approached the tee, a rotund man smoking a cigarette waited in a top-of-the-line golf cart.

"Hey, Mr. Sutcliffe." Tommy parked next to him. "How are you?"

"Fine." Mr. Sutcliffe took a drag on his cigarette and hauled himself out of the cart. "Seems like we always get backed up on this hole. Even if the course isn't busy." He motioned toward the foursome in the fairway.

"I'm sorry, sir." Concern creased Tommy's brow.

He glanced at his gold watch. "I'm supposed to meet Caterina for dinner at eight." He took his driver from his golf bag.

"Mr. Sutcliffe, this is my girlfriend Laura Patterson and her friend Georgia Winston."

"Ladies, this is Don Sutcliffe, Zenith's grandpa."

"Nice to meet you," Laura and I said in unison.

Don aimed a curt nod in our direction as he ambled to the tee.

"I'm surprised you don't have a caddie with you, sir," Tommy said. "Were we not able to accommodate you? If so, I apologize, and we'll make it up to you."

It was completely fascinating watching Tommy kiss up to this man. I'd never imagined he could be so—*deferential.*

"Nope. Needed to be alone to think." Don tossed his cigarette into the grass, and with a decisive swing, sent the ball soaring along the right side of the fairway.

"Nice shot, sir," Tommy said. "And I'm very sorry about Aaron."

Don bent and swiped his cigarette. "Me too. My grandson shouldn't have to grow up without a father." He shoved it back in his mouth as he lumbered back to his cart.

Laura and I exchanged glances. *Ew.* Weren't there chemicals on that thing? But why worry about that when you were inhaling nicotine?

"Enjoy the rest of your round." Don started to drive away but slammed the brakes. The cart beeped as he drove in reverse and stopped next to Tommy. "I heard what happened with Craig at the marina the other day."

"Oh really?" Tommy sounded—and appeared—so completely innocent that I almost laughed out loud.

Don chuckled without sounding amused. "One of the guys that works for me gave me a heads up, and I watched the security camera footage." He tossed his cigarette butt into the grass. "I had a long talk with my son about our customer service expectations. Don't feel you need to keep your distance. My granddaughter's father is welcome any time."

"Thank you, sir. Zenith loves the candy, and I'm pleased with my Sea-Doo."

"Excellent." He drove away.

The mention of the Sea-Doo caused a wave of guilt to wash over me. Laura deserved to know what'd happened to me earlier, especially since it involved her WaveRunner. "Someone driving a BlackBlaze 8200 chased me today when I was out on your Wave-Runner," I blurted.

"What!" Laura slid out of their cart.

I explained what had happened and how I'd gotten names of BlackBlaze owners from Keith Thurston and searched for connections with no luck. Tommy clenched his fists, and Laura gaped at me.

"I did send Detective McCloud the list," I said.

"Good," Laura said. "You need to be careful, so no more investigating. You don't owe Sheila Thurston a single thing, and her son isn't even a suspect. If she wants answers, she can nose around and get them for herself."

"That's for sure." As Tommy stared toward Mr. Sutcliffe,

who was hitting his second shot in the fairway, his gaze grew contemplative.

"You look like you have a thought." I slapped a mosquito on my arm.

"Sutcliffe Marina ain't a BlackBlaze dealer, but with their connections, if Craig wanted to take one out for a spin, he probably could. Or someone brought in a BlackBlaze to trade, and Craig was taking it for a test run."

"Where does Craig live?" I asked.

"Calloway Cove," Tommy said.

"When I was on the WaveRunner, I did some three-sixties back there, so maybe he saw me."

"Could be." Tommy walked to the tee. "I'm gonna have to do some investigating of my own. If that punk's involved, I'll make sure my ex keeps Zenith away from that psycho. Not that Nora will listen to my opinion, because she's got a huge blind spot where her brother's concerned." He hit the ball, and it sliced into the trees.

I was slightly proud that I'd learned the correct terminology.

He grimaced as he put away his driver. "Worst shot of the day. Ladies, it looks like it's up to you. I'm going bananas thinking 'bout my little girl's crazy uncle hurting somebody."

"Excuses, excuses." I slipped my golf ball into the washer.

He pointed at me. "Can't blame a man for trying."

Once we were finished golfing, Laura and I freshened up in the ladies' locker room before we met Tommy in the country club's dining room.

The host seated us next to the floor-to-ceiling windows, which gave us a perfect view of the lake's glistening water—and the sinking sun. Tommy and Laura insisted I take the seat facing the lake. I wasn't thrilled about sitting with my back to the restaurant, but I didn't argue.

One table over, Don Sutcliffe sat with a woman that I assumed was his wife—since he'd mentioned meeting her for dinner. Deep trenches rimmed her weary blue eyes, and her gray hair was gathered in a ponytail. She was dressed in a Hideaway 5K T-shirt, jeans, and a running shoe. She wore a walking boot on her right foot.

As I studied the menu, I couldn't help but overhear Don and Caterina talking. Okay, so I could've helped it if I'd focused on Tommy and Laura's conversation about what they were ordering for dinner and what they would share, but that wasn't exactly riveting information. I glanced at Don and Caterina out of the corner of my eye.

"Dee won't listen. I tried talking to her again today." Caterina sipped from a wine glass.

Don sighed. "I'm sure she'll be fine. She's young, and the midwife is experienced."

"I don't understand why you're taking her side."

Don drained his amber-colored drink and slammed it against the table. "This isn't about taking sides. It's about respecting our daughter's wishes."

"Even if her wishes might cause her death—or the baby's?"

"Women have been giving birth at home for years, and Dee's pregnancy isn't high-risk."

"Please talk to her again." She moved some lettuce around her salad plate. "She listens to you. Our family doesn't need another tragedy."

"I'll see if I can convince her to use a birthing center in Fort Wayne," Don said. "Would that make you feel better?"

"Not really." Her lips flattened as she glared at her husband. "It's still not a hospital."

"But it's a compromise."

"Earth to Georgia." Laura surveyed me with a frown. "Are you ready to order?"

I closed the menu and glanced at our amused waiter. "I'll take the parmesan-crusted chicken."

"Is everything all right?" Tommy asked after the waiter walked away. "You looked like you were taking a mental field trip to Mars."

Oh, how he made me long for a spaceship to another planet. "Sure. There were too many good things to choose from on the menu."

"You got that right." He patted his belly. "I've gotta be careful, so I stay fit for my girl." He took Laura's hand, and she beamed.

"Oh. My. Goodness," Laura whispered. "Don't turn around, but Governor Milton just walked in." She appeared as if she were suppressing the urge to squeal.

I didn't give a hoot about Michigan politics, even if this guy might run for president someday, so taking her word about his arrival was no problem. I might've cared a teeny bit more if the Indiana governor had arrived—but not much.

However, Don Sutcliffe apparently cared—a lot—because while his wife was talking, he jumped up, tossed his napkin on the table, and practically threw himself at the politician as he passed their table. Caterina smiled tightly and stabbed her salad.

"Darwin! Good to see you." Don clasped the governor's hand.

"How's your golf game?" Governor Milton asked.

"Mediocre at best."

Governor Milton guffawed. "I don't believe you. You've always handled yourself like a pro on the links."

"You have time for a round tomorrow?" Don asked.

Governor Milton consulted his phone. "How about seven-thirty? Nothing like starting the day on the links. I'll ask Byron to join us."

"Perfect. I'll see you then. Enjoy your dinner." Don rejoined his glaring wife as the governor waved at Tommy before strolling to the bar.

"I wish you wouldn't play golf with that man." Caterina picked up her knife and sliced a beet. "After the way he cheated on his wife."

"Who cheated on him first, if I recall."

"Two wrongs don't make a right."

"Those indiscretions happened a long time ago." Don spread his napkin in his lap. "He's a changed man."

She sniffed. "Politicians never change."

Amen, sister.

Half an hour later, the Sutcliffes had left the country club's dining room, the sun had sunk below the horizon, and we'd just finished our strawberry shortcake when Tommy snapped his fingers.

"I know why Valerie Hudson's name sounds familiar." He stood and tossed his napkin on the table. "Follow me." He directed Laura and me down the hallway that led to the locker rooms. The wall to our right had windows with a view of the golf course. The wall on our left was adorned with framed photos of golfers and tennis players. Aaron's wife Dee had won the club championship for women's golf four years earlier.

Interesting.

Tommy stopped and pointed at a photo of a pretty girl with dark hair. She stood on a tennis court and held a trophy. "Valerie Hudson. Club Champion in the women's tennis tournament seven years ago. That was before my time, or I might've remembered her name sooner."

"Good work, Tommy." I took a picture. The next time I saw Clover, I'd have her confirm Valerie's identity.

"Forget Tom-Tom." Laura kissed his cheek. "I'll have to call you Sherlock."

"Eh. How about Magnum P.I.? Tom Selleck, of course." He squared his shoulders.

"Oohh. Even better," Laura cooed.

"I could grow a mustache."

"Maybe." Laura's enthusiasm took a nosedive.

I gave stern orders for my eyes not to roll but didn't bother stifling my laugh as the show's theme song played in my head. Magnum was a perfect nickname.

Tommy certainly had the chest hair for it.

The next morning, Gus and I had just returned from a walk to the beach when my phone buzzed with a call from Laura, who was at work.

"What's going on?" I shut the patio door behind us and unhooked Gus's leash.

Panting, he took off for his water dish in the corner of the kitchen and slurped loudly.

"Good news about Aaron's case. The sheriff's department made an arrest about an hour ago."

My eyes bugged. "Who?"

"Craig Sutcliffe."

CHAPTER FIFTEEN

"Wow." I was *slightly* disappointed Detective McCloud and the Webster County Sheriff's Department had solved the case without my assistance, but justice for Aaron was all that mattered. "What're you allowed to tell me?"

"Your tip about the BlackBlaze helped," Laura said.

"How?"

"One of the owners, Danielle DuPont, lives with her boyfriend Mike—who's Craig's neighbor. Mike and Danielle are in Europe for a wedding, and since they live on Calloway Cove, Craig could've borrowed their BlackBlaze without anyone knowing, and we think he saw you and decided to warn you. He doesn't have an alibi for yesterday afternoon, and nobody knows why he wasn't at work."

"Why'd he kill Aaron?"

Gus wandered over and stared at me, so I tossed him a rope toy, and he gnawed away.

"Don *was* going to put Aaron in charge of the marina to clean up Craig's mess, and he was jealous. Evidently, Craig waited for

Aaron while he was out running, bashed him in the head, and dumped his body in the lake."

I considered the texts from Aaron that Keith Thurston had shown me. He'd made it sound more like Aaron and Craig were coconspirators—not enemies. Why would Craig have wanted to kill Aaron when he was helping? It might not matter, but I had to tell Laura. "Last night, I forgot—"

"Sorry, but I've got to go." Someone was talking in the background. "This information is going to be released to the public, so if you need to get Sheila off your back, feel free to tell her."

"I—"

"I'll be home around five. You and Gus have fun today."

She disconnected, and I scowled at the phone. But this wasn't my problem. Obviously, Detective McCloud had evidence I didn't know about, and Laura couldn't tell me everything. Tossing my phone aside, I went out and found Sheila weeding her landscaping.

Her eyes grew enormous as I updated her. "What a shame," she said. "I knew Craig had a temper, but I didn't think he was capable of cold-blooded murder. I guess you never know about people."

"No—you really don't." I'd learned that the hard way.

"What are you up to today?" She pushed her poufy gray hair out of her face.

"Well . . . I've been meaning to ask . . . would you mind if Gus and I took your paddle boat for a spin around the channel before it gets too hot?"

"Not at all." She tossed a weed aside. "I'm headed to the grocery, so I'm not going to need it. Have a good time."

Back when I was a kid, my brother Dakota and I always loved taking Grandma and Grandpa's paddle boat for a ride so Dakota could catch turtles. While Mom or Daddy and I propelled the boat, Dakota sat poised with a net, ready to spring and capture any hapless turtles who were sunning themselves on logs. Most of the time, the larger—and wiser—turtles evaded imprisonment because they dove into the water long before we floated up. Baby turtles weren't so smart, and Dakota was able to snare quite a few, though Mom always made him release them before we returned home.

As I enjoyed these memories, Gus, in his doggie life vest, sat beside me, and I pedaled down Laura's channel. We should've taken the ride in the morning, because now the sun was roasting us. Gus panted, and I adjusted my Colts cap. At least there was a breeze that made the heat bearable.

Though the case was wrapped up, I couldn't stop thinking about Craig's motive. Even if Craig was furious about being usurped, he'd killed the man who was supposed to swoop in and save his family's marina—and livelihood. That didn't make sense unless Don was planning to completely cut Craig out as punishment.

Unless Craig was crazy. After seeing him take a swing at Tommy, I considered that a strong possibility.

But how many times in a few days had I wanted to take a swing at Tommy? Yeah. That wasn't the best indicator of a person's sanity.

Skimming my hand across the water's smooth surface, I glided past lily pads. The swoosh-swoosh, swoosh-swoosh of the boat had a hypnotic effect. "I'm disappointed I couldn't contribute, Gus, but I guess, in a way, I did, since I reported being chased."

Gus thumped his tail against the seat and sniffed the air. I wrinkled my nose as a fishy smell invaded my nostrils.

Why should I care about the fate of a guy who'd tried to run me down? I didn't. But if Craig was the wrong guy, then the killer was still free.

We reached the lake, and waves jostled the boat. I turned to head back toward Laura's house, and as I moved away from the lake, my phone rang with a number I didn't recognize.

Not wanting to shatter the peace, I left the phone in the cupholder and pedaled on.

As soon as the ringing stopped, it started again.

Good grief. Had one of my stepbrothers gotten a new number? Both Preston and Austin had a habit of calling until I answered, but they'd backed off on that annoying practice since we'd been getting along better.

I grabbed the phone. "Hello?"

"It's Tommy. I thought you were never gonna answer."

I should've known. I stopped pedaling and drifted. Ahead of me, a few sunning turtles dove off a log. They must've met my brother.

"What's going on?"

"Craig was arrested for Aaron Lehman's murder."

"I heard."

"He didn't do it."

"What!" I sat up straighter, and the boat bumped into a log. "A couple of days ago you told me you suspected him, and last night you were saying how crazy he is, and you were worried about Zenith."

"He is. But he ain't dumb. Zenith's mom Nora swears he's innocent of Aaron's murder, and she's got a point. Craig confessed to Nora that he'd made a mess of the business, and Aaron was going to help him straighten it out. Why would he kill someone who was doing that?"

I drew my fingers through the murky water. "I admit the same thought crossed my mind."

"I knew you and me would be on the same page."

"I don't know about—"

"Craig doesn't have an alibi for the night somebody offed Aaron, so now he's gonna hang for Aaron's murder while the real killer gets away. Craig's convinced someone's trying to frame him."

"Does he have any idea who?"

"No."

Of course he didn't. I stroked Gus's head. "Why are you so willing to help him?"

"I don't want my girl's uncle going to jail for a crime he didn't commit. I've got some shady characters on my side of the family, but nobody's killed anybody. I don't want her gettin' a bad reputation because of her uncle. Besides, God saved me, and now I work for him. And I'm sure God wants me to help Craig."

I felt a little good-old-fashioned conviction of my own. No. It was more like a lightning bolt of conviction. I'd been way too hard on Tommy. "I understand."

"So you'll help?"

I pedaled. "Yes." I might as well admit I wasn't meant to have a vacation.

"That's awesome. Thanks, sweetheart! I'll swing by in fifteen minutes to pick you up."

"Wait. Where're we going?" I floated to Sheila's pier and grabbed the wooden slats.

"To see Craig. In jail." He disconnected.

Tommy arrived in less than fifteen minutes, and I'd barely had time to eat a peanut butter sandwich, change clothes, and rebraid my fuzzy hair. I decided it was safer for all concerned if I left my baseball cap on.

I let him in. "I'm not sure we'll be allowed to see Craig."

"We've got to try. How would you feel if the wrong person got put away for your dad's murder and the real psycho was running around free as a bird?" He followed me into the kitchen.

He'd known me for a few days and had already figured out my weak spot. *Well played, Tommy Ferraro. Well played.* "Fine." I took a water bottle from the fridge. "Let's get this over with."

Tommy's phone blasted *The Brady Bunch* theme song.

I raised my eyebrows.

"What? It was my favorite show as a kid. I watched reruns every day after school. Z loves it too." He answered, but as he listened, his pleasant expression faded. "No *way.*" He paused and shifted back and forth. "All right. I'm sorry. Yeah. I'll come get her." He disconnected and slapped his palm against the counter.

"What's wrong?"

"That was Nora. Craig's on his way to the hospital."

I sat on the bar stool. "What happened?"

"They think it's a heart attack." Tommy set his phone on the peninsula with a sigh. "I hate to say it, but you saw him. He's overweight. Ticking time bomb."

I cringed and twisted the cap off my water bottle. "I'm sure the stress of getting arrested didn't help." I took a drink.

"Exactly. *Kaboom!*" Tommy shook his head. "Plan B. How about you come with me and talk to Nora when I pick up Zenith? See if she knows anything that might help."

"Sure. No problem." At least—I hoped it wouldn't be.

"What happened to your other girlfriend, Tommy?" The blond woman, whom I assumed was Nora because of her resemblance to her sister Dee, surveyed me as Tommy and I stood on the front porch of her Hidden Shores bungalow.

"Nothing," Tommy said. "She's working. This is her friend Georgia. Georgia, this is my baby mama, Nora."

Nora's eyes were red, and her mascara had smudged. She was pretty in an artificial way and wore a denim romper.

"I'm so sorry about Craig," I said.

"Thanks. Come in." She stepped aside. "Z's in her room." She closed the door and eyed me again.

I took in the cozy, toy-covered living space. Though the house was small, the furnishings and décor looked expensive.

"Georgia's gonna help us figure out who's framing Craig," Tommy said, as if he could read his ex-girlfriend's thoughts. "You got a minute to chat?"

She swiped her nose with a wadded tissue. "If we make it quick. Dee will be here any minute to drive us to the hospital."

"Of course," I said.

"Are you with the police?" She motioned to the sofa, and I had a seat amongst the Barbie clothes scattered on the cushions.

"Georgia's solved some cases in her hometown." Tommy picked up a pink, sparkly Barbie dress and dropped it on the coffee table before he sat.

"Right. Well good luck with this one. My brother has a talent for ticking people off." She studied her pointy yellow nails. "After Craig was arrested, he called and told me to get a hold of our family's lawyer. We didn't talk long, but he swore up and down he didn't kill Aaron and that he was relieved Aaron was going to help straighten out the mess he'd made of the business." She rolled her eyes. "I love my brother, but Dad *never* should've put Craig in charge. Dee and I weren't interested, but we'd have had enough sense not to run the marina into the ground."

"Can you think of anyone who'd want to frame your brother?" I asked.

"His ex-girlfriends?" Nora fiddled with her romper's hem.

"Again. I love him, but he's a lousy boyfriend and has terrible taste in women."

"Any woman in particular?" I asked.

"He's dated a lot of girls, but only one is truly cray-cray."

"Which one?"

She narrowed her eyes. "Clover Calloway—the ice cream chick."

CHAPTER SIXTEEN

"Craig *dated* Clover?" I graded myself at a solid F minus for tact because I couldn't quite keep from being shocked at the thought of them as a couple. But if she'd been after his family's money . . .

"She sure did," Nora said. "They met when he was volunteering at the animal shelter."

"Why'd they break up?" I asked.

"He gave her a gorgeous diamond pendant for her birthday." Nora scowled. "Then, he found out she sold the diamond and replaced it with cubic zirconia. After that, he had enough of her shenanigans."

"Did she ever tell him why she sold the diamond?"

"She wanted to pay off her ice cream truck." Nora huffed.

Sheila's description of Clover as a money grubber seemed spot on. "It's tacky, but I wouldn't call it crazy," I said. "Especially if she was struggling to pay for the truck."

"I might agree if it weren't for the obituary she wrote for him."

"What?" Had I heard Nora correctly?

"This ought to be good," Tommy muttered.

"Yep. Crazy Clover wrote an obituary for Craig and put it in his birthday card," Nora said.

I glanced at Tommy, whose mouth had dropped open. "Nothing says happy birthday like an obituary," I said.

"I know, right?" Nora rolled her eyes. "My sister and I both told Craig to get rid of her then, but he gave us some song and dance about Clover inspiring him to think about how he'd want to be remembered." She crossed her arms. "Her reasons didn't matter. It was creepy—and nuts. Still, he put up with her until the diamond incident. It wouldn't surprise me one bit if she killed Aaron just to frame my brother. She was pretty upset when Craig dumped her. I figure she was sorry to see a potential sugar daddy get away."

"Did Clover have anything against Aaron?" I asked.

"No. But that doesn't mean anything when a person's nuts."

The front door creaked open, and Dee ambled inside. She surveyed all of us, but her eyes bored into me. "You are?"

"Georgia Winston."

"My girlfriend's detective buddy," Tommy added. "We're helping Craig."

She leaned against the couch. "He needs all the help he can get."

"I'm sorry for your loss," I said.

"Me too," Dee whispered and rested her hand on her belly. "I've been living a nightmare the last few days." With teary eyes, she looked at her sister. "What'd I walk in on?"

"I was telling them about our brother dating Crazy Clover."

"She's got a screw loose, for sure," Dee said.

"How long ago did they break up?" I asked.

Nora glanced at Dee. "Last summer?"

"That sounds right." Dee brushed her bangs aside.

That seemed like a long time for Clover to wait before taking revenge. "Clover needs a closer look, so I'll do some digging."

If she'd killed Aaron and wanted to frame Craig, then he would've been an easy target. Clover probably knew Danielle DuPont and could've gotten her hands on the BlackBlaze. After all, she hadn't been at her ice cream truck when I'd been chased down, and Craig's neighborhood was within walking distance of Lakeview Park—or her friend in the VW van could've dropped her off.

I turned to Dee. "I hate to ask, but do you believe your brother killed your husband?"

"No way. Craig's too lazy to pull off a mur—" Dee squeezed her eyes shut and pressed her fist to her mouth. "You're on the right track with the Clover thing." She opened her eyes and stood. "Excuse me. I need to use the bathroom before we leave." She waddled out of the room.

"I'll get Zenith, so you two can get going," Tommy said.

As Nora stacked Barbie clothes on the coffee table, silence fell over the room, and I wasn't going to wait around for it to get uncomfortable.

"You mentioned Craig had made a mess of the family business. What happened?" I wanted to see what she'd tell me.

"He had a lot of personal credit card debt he wanted to pay off. So he paid himself more and went cheap when he hired employees. The new mechanic did a crappy job. Craig wasn't maintaining the building like he should've. I warned dad, but he was content to let Craig make his own mistakes." She closed her fist around a Barbie dress. "I won't lie. My brother has a lot of issues, but deep down, he has a good heart."

I stood. "If you think of anything else, please call me." I handed her a business card.

"Thanks. One more thing." She leaned closer. "That friend of yours, Laura?"

"Yes?" I braced myself for where Nora was going.

"Z likes her. Would she be a good stepmother?" She scooped up the remaining Barbie clothes and dumped them in a pink plastic case.

"Definitely. She babysat a lot when we were in high school and has always wanted kids. From what I've witnessed, she cares about Zenith."

"Good." She set the case on a toy shelf. "Tommy's dated a couple of other women I wasn't crazy about, but I'm thinking Laura is good for him—if he doesn't blow it. Supposedly, he's found God, so hopefully that'll make a difference in how he treats women." She sat a Barbie next to the case. "All I know is that we were a disaster as a couple, so I'm perfectly content to co-parent, and he's a good daddy to Z." She straightened the magazines on her coffee table. "Do you have a boyfriend?"

"Yes."

"What's he do?"

"He's an actor."

Nora sniffed. "Good luck with that. I dated an actor back when I lived in L.A. with my sister. He cared more about his career than me." She fluffed a couple of pillows. "But maybe things are different in your case."

I wasn't so sure.

Tommy dropped me off at Laura's with the promise to return later to pick us up for dinner, but I wasn't convinced any of us would feel like going out.

I called Hamlet, and when he didn't answer, I flopped on the bed with a sigh. It was fine. I couldn't expect him to be available at all times. As much fun as I'd had visiting Laura, I was ready to go home. It'd be good to sleep in my own bed, see my family and other friends, and get my regular fix at Latte Conspiracies. I wouldn't even mind getting back to work on the farm.

"Are you homesick, Gus?"

He dropped to the floor, rested his chin on his paws, and looked at me. I interpreted this as a solid yes.

I was about to go downstairs to Laura's office and spin a few theories when Hamlet called.

"Are you staying safe?" he asked.

"Sort of. Except for the crazy person who chased me until I fell off Laura's WaveRunner."

He gasped. "What?"

I explained what'd happened yesterday afternoon, and as I told him, I realized I should've called him last night. But he could've checked in with me. The Hamlet of two months ago would've. I tried to push the thought away—and couldn't.

"When are you coming home?" he asked.

"Probably tomorrow. The side ditches aren't going to mow themselves." I stared at the whirling ceiling fan.

"Good. I'll be glad to see you. What's happening with the case?"

I filled him in on Craig's arrest and how I wasn't convinced he'd murdered Aaron in the first place. I finished with Clover's antics because that was a fitting finale.

"I'd avoid buying any more ice cream from her," he said.

"That's the plan." I propped my head up with a throw pillow. "How're rehearsals?"

"Great. And I have some other exciting news. Do you remember me talking about my friend Phil who's an indie filmmaker?"

"In Chicago?" My stomach tightened.

"Yes. He's asked me to audition for a role in a movie he's directing."

"What about *The Music Man?*" I sat up.

"If I get the part—and there are certainly no guarantees—we wouldn't start filming until October after the musical's run is over."

"That's cool. I didn't know you were interested in making movies." I sounded positive, didn't I?

"I didn't think I was either, but the more I've thought about it, the more I realized I want to try."

I ran my hand over the comforter. "When's your audition?"

"Tomorrow. Don't worry. Even if I get the part and have to go to Chicago temporarily, I won't forget about you." He chuckled.

Why did he feel the need to tack on a statement that was about a hundred miles from reassuring? "I know."

But I really didn't.

"Do you truly believe Craig killed Aaron?" I asked Laura that evening after she came home from work and found me standing in her office. I'd added Clover's name to the suspect board.

She tossed her briefcase on her desk. "That's what the evidence suggests, and Ryan's case is solid. I see you don't agree." A hint of irritation crept into her tone as she pointed at the whiteboard before dropping onto her couch and tucking her legs under her black, palm print skirt.

"I might. If Tommy and I hadn't talked to Nora Sutcliffe and Dee Lehman this afternoon."

"How did that happen?"

"Tommy asked me to go with him to get Zenith so I could talk to Nora."

"Because he believed the line his ex-girlfriend fed him about her poor brother." She crossed her arms.

"Nora freely admits Craig has done a terrible job managing the marina but doesn't believe he killed Aaron. Dee doesn't buy it either. Says Craig's too lazy to murder someone."

"You wouldn't want to believe it either if your brother were arrested."

"True." I couldn't figure out if Laura was more upset over me hanging out with Tommy—not that she had any reason to worry about me stealing her man—or if she was ticked that I was questioning law enforcement.

"Why'd you add Clover's name?" she asked.

"Craig dated her."

Laura's eyes bugged. "No. Way."

"Yes way." I gave Laura the run-down, including Nora and Dee's opinions of Clover. I didn't mention Nora asking about Laura, because clearly, she wasn't in the mood to hear about that little conversation. By the time I'd finished, I wished I'd taken a picture of Laura's face when I told her about Clover and the obituary.

Laura squinted at the board. "The obituary stunt is bizarre on a level I can't fathom, but I don't see anything that changes my mind about Ryan's conclusion that Craig is Aaron's killer."

"Has Detective McCloud even looked at Clover? She could've chased me with the BlackBlaze since she wasn't running her ice cream truck at the time, and as Craig's ex-girlfriend, she probably knew his neighbor's girlfriend had a BlackBlaze. Plus, we can't forget that she may have lied about Aaron selling drugs."

"Uggghhh! Georgia. Give. It. Up. Craig's the guy!" She drove her fist into a throw pillow. "I could throttle Tommy for dragging you back into this," she muttered. "You were supposed to be having a relaxing vacation."

"I'm sorry." I capped the marker and sat on the couch.

"No. *I'm* sorry. Nora gives Tommy a sob story about her nutcase brother and his crazy ex-girlfriend, and he believes her!"

"If it makes you feel better, Tommy cares more about clearing Craig's name—for Zenith's sake. It's not about Nora."

"So he says."

We sat in silence, staring at the board. Did Laura and Tommy have a future if she couldn't trust his dealings with Zenith's mother? But now wasn't the time for me to ask that question.

I looked back at our notes. "Have you heard any more about what caused Byron and Minnie's boat to explode?"

"The new fuel line was faulty, and gasoline leaked into the bilge. A spark caused the explosion."

"More incompetence from Sutcliffe Marina?"

"Exactly. Byron's planning to sue over it." Laura stood. "Are you up for pizza tonight? There's a great little place in downtown Hidden Shores that Tommy and Zenith love. Their breadsticks are amazing."

"Absolutely. Breadsticks make everything better."

She smiled wryly. "That's one thing we can agree on."

Before we left to get pizza that evening, I did a little reconnaissance in hopes of avoiding Sheila—and Pickles. She and her feline companion were lurking in her screened-in porch, but just to make sure she hadn't somehow materialized in the front yard during the time it took me to walk through Laura's house, I peeked out the door. Her garage door was closed, but a motorcycle was parked in her driveway.

"The coast is clear, Gus."

He led me outside, and when he finished his business, I turned to go into Laura's house. Out of the corner of my eye, I caught sight of a familiar Jeep approaching. The driver honked and turned into the driveway.

I backed onto the porch and bonked my head against the hanging basket of petunias. It couldn't be. Rubbing my head, I blinked, and Gus woofed. *Why would . . . ?*

Cal stepped out of the Jeep. "Hey, Georgia."

CHAPTER SEVENTEEN

I reached for the porch railing to steady myself as my heart flopped. A grin spread over Cal's face as he strolled up the driveway.

Oh, how I'd missed his dimple.

Gus shot forward, dragging me from the porch, and I stumbled off the last step.

Merciful heavens.

When I regained my balance, I tugged on the leash, but Gus jumped up and greeted Cal, who clasped the dog's paws.

"Hey there, buddy." Cal's blue eyes twinkled. "Did you miss your neighbor?"

Gus wagged his tail and licked Cal's hand.

At least Gus had taken the heat off of my graceful stumble. "Down, Gus."

"He's fine." Cal dropped the dog's feet and met my gaze. His broad shoulders, muscular chest, and tall frame had always made me forget I was too tall for my own good.

And he was gorgeous. The kind of handsome that made a girl

want to swoon—and I'd never been mistaken for the delicate type.

But I already had a wonderful and handsome boyfriend, so I needed to stop.

Immediately.

"What brings you to the lake?" I managed to squeak out. Really, I was acting ridiculous. There was no way I should be having this sort of reaction to a man who'd pushed me away—even if his motive had been honorable.

Get a grip, Georgia Rae.

"Vanessa's in-laws have a place on Hideaway, and she and Curtis are here on vacation. They invited me for the day."

I pushed away the thought that it would be fun to hang out with Cal's partner and her husband. "Cool. Laura's neighbor knows Curtis." I motioned toward Keith's house and cringed inwardly at our stilted conversation. How had Cal and I ever managed to date?

"Anyway. I thought I'd stop here on my way home." He ran his hands through his dark hair. "Is there somewhere we could talk?" His sexy, resonant voice was dead serious. For about two seconds, I thought I detected a hint of apprehension in his expression.

"Sure. Laura and I are going to get pizza in a bit with her boyfriend and his daughter." My voice sounded a lot less squeaky, which was good because there was absolutely no reason for me to be acting like a middle school girl with a crush.

"That sounds fun."

"Yep." We filed inside where I released Gus, but as if he sensed my need for emotional support, he stayed by my side. "Have a seat." I pointed at the sofa. "I'll tell Laura you're here."

Gus, who wasn't the emotional support animal that I'd hoped, followed Cal and rested at his feet when he sat on the couch.

Traitor.

I stalked to Laura's bedroom and knocked on the door. When she told me to come in, I darted inside, slammed the door, and stood pressed against it. "Cal's here."

She emerged from her bathroom with a makeup palette in one hand and a brush in the other. "Why?"

"I have no idea. He asked if there was some place we could talk, and he looked serious. Maybe he's checking on me because the other night when he sent me the pictures of his kitchen, I told him about finding Aaron's body, and I guess I shouldn't have, but it just slipped out. Anyway, I just wanted to tell you he was here, so you didn't come walking out in your underwear or something like that. Not that you walk around in your underwear, but if you happened to make a quick run to get that cute little top from your drying rack in the utility room and he was sitting in there that could be really embarrassing especially since you've never met, and—"

"Georgia Rae Winston." She chuckled. "I promise I won't walk out in my unmentionables." She pointed at her denim shorts and sparkly gray tank top. "See. Already dressed."

"Right. I thought I should inform you of the guest since it's your house and—"

"Why are you so nervous?" She snapped her palette shut.

"Nervous? I'm not nervous. Why do you think I'm nervous?" *Because you're acting like a kid caught snooping for birthday presents, Georgia the Genius.* I gasped. "What if something happened to someone in my family or to one of my friends, and he's here to tell me in person?" My stomach dropped. But he'd been visiting Vanessa and Curtis, so that couldn't be it, right?

"Go see what he wants. I'll be in here if you need me."

"You don't want to meet him?"

"After seeing you react this way, I'm starting to feel sorry for Hamlet and *definitely* want to meet Cal, but first, you need to figure out what he's doing here." She waved her hand at the door. "Shoo. I'll make an appearance in a few minutes."

"Right." I turned and marched back to the living room.

Cal's forehead creased with concern. "What's wrong?" Gus, who hadn't left his post at Cal's feet, raised his head.

"Did something happen to my family or friends?"

"No. I should've made that clear. I'm sorry for scaring you."

"It's okay." I dropped onto the opposite end of the sofa. "Then why are you here?"

"I owe you an apology." He looked me straight in the eyes. "I've been wanting to say something to you for a while, and I've been putting it off." He shifted. "I was going to talk to you at home, but when I got on the highway, God was bugging me about saying something now, so I turned around, found Laura's address, and . . ."

Seconds ticked by, and I really, really, *really* wanted to stop the silence with a torrent of words. But deep in my gut, I knew I needed to keep my mouth shut and let Cal say whatever it was he needed to say.

He smoothed his khaki shorts. "Remember how I went to see Mason in Atlanta a few months ago?"

"Yes."

"While I was there, he told me that even though he'd never understand why Natalie had to die that way, he realized it wasn't his fault, and he'd never regret the time he had with her."

"I'm glad. It'd be easy for him to blame himself."

"Right. It's taken him a while to get to that point. But seeing Mason made me realize . . . if I believe God's in control, then I need to act like it. Pushing you away because I was afraid something would happen to you like it did to Natalie was wrong." He stared at Laura's fireplace. "We both know trusting God doesn't mean we're free from bad things happening."

A lump formed in my throat as I thought of Daddy.

"But we can't reject the good things God gives us just because we're afraid of losing them."

My gut clenched. Why hadn't Cal realized this sooner?

"Georgia, I'm sorry. I know you're with Hamlet, and I've lost my chance with you. I'm not asking you to change anything. He's a great guy, and I meant what I said when I told you he'd be good for you. I want more than anything for you to be happy."

"Thank you," I whispered. "I'm sorry I demanded answers—and that I was so nosy about your feelings."

"You were being reasonable and had every right to know where our relationship was going. I was wrong for telling you my life wasn't a mystery that needed to be solved. I was stupid for pushing you away and not trusting God with our future. I was an idiot for not telling you how much I loved you." He reached out and took both of my hands. "Please forgive me."

As thankful as I was for his apology that I'd longed to hear but hadn't realized how much I needed to hear, I could only focus on one word.

Loved.

Not love.

Cal wasn't asking for anything but my forgiveness. My nose burned, and I swallowed hard. "I forgive you." I truly meant it.

But it didn't free me from the suffocating sadness that'd taken up residence in my heart.

Again.

He squeezed my hands. "Thank you."

Laura poked her head around the corner. "Is everything okay in here?"

CHAPTER EIGHTEEN

C al stood. "Yes. Everything's fine." He crossed the room, held out his hand, and dimpled as if his load had been lightened. "Detective Cal Perkins."

Sure. Everything was hunky-dory for him.

Laura glanced at me as she grasped his hand. "Laura Patterson. What brings you to Lake Hideaway?"

"I'll let Georgia tell you." He glanced at his watch. "I need to get back to Wildcat Springs."

She looked back and forth between us. "You're welcome to stay and get pizza with us."

I wasn't sure why she felt like extending an invitation to him to stay when the tension in the room was a thousand times more suffocating than the July humidity.

"Thanks, but I really can't. I have to work tomorrow." He headed for the door.

"Tommy's running late, so no hurry." Laura sidestepped toward her back porch. "I'll be out there if you need me." She snagged Gus's collar and hurried outside in a clumsy, un-Laura-like manner.

I hauled myself off the couch and followed Cal to the foyer.

"When are you heading home?" He opened the door, and we walked outside.

Why should he care? "Possibly tomorrow."

Maybe instead of going home, I'd drive west with Gus until I reached the Pacific. I'd hop a plane to Hawaii and live out my days as a spinster in solitude, farming pineapples and eating fresh fish that I caught with a handmade fishing pole. I wouldn't be completely alone. I'd have Gus to keep me company, and he'd love the warm weather and frolicking on the beach.

"Georgia?"

I managed a fake smile. "Sorry." *Just babbling in my head.* "Have a safe trip."

His dimple made an appearance as he got in his Jeep. "I'll see you around." He gave a friendly wave as he drove away.

I went to the kitchen, filled a glass with water, and cupped my hands around it.

"Are you all right?" Laura peeked in around the porch door.

Gus nudged his way inside and checked on me by rubbing his nose all over my denim capri pants.

"Yeah."

"You don't have to go with us tonight."

"I want to. It'll be fun." I forced myself to swallow more water. It was perfectly obvious Laura was dying to know what'd happened between Cal and me, and as freaked out as I was, there was no point in trying to fool her. "Cal came to ask my forgiveness." I recapped the conversation.

"Wow." She narrowed her eyes. "Why do you look like you're about ten seconds away from having a major meltdown?"

I clenched my jaw. "He finally admitted he loved me. *Loved.* As in past tense."

She crossed her arms. "He knows you're dating Hamlet. If

he's the stand-up guy that you've led me to believe he is, do you expect him to come here and try to steal another man's girl?"

"If he still loved me, he might."

"Do you think it's possible he loves you but doesn't want to admit it because he thinks you're happy with Hamlet?"

"So he's pushing me away again."

"No. He thinks he's doing the noble thing."

"Which is exactly what he was doing before. So in spite of today's grand gesture, we haven't made any progress."

Laura groaned and muttered something under her breath. "Can I assume from this conversation that you're still in love with Cal?"

I wanted to hide in a corner. "I don't know. It doesn't matter. I'm with Hamlet now."

"Georgia Rae Winston! You can't stay with Hamlet if you're in love with Cal."

"I can if I'm in love with Hamlet."

"Are you?"

I buried my face in my hands. "I don't know," I wailed.

"Yes. You do."

I lifted my head and met her prosecutorial stare.

"You just don't want to admit it."

Because of her own rough day and my drama, Laura made the executive decision to cancel our trip to town, and we had a pizza delivered instead. Since Tommy hadn't had a great day either, he chose to stay home and enjoy his time with Zenith. After scarfing down a supreme pizza, Laura and I binged on ice cream and *Murder, She Wrote* episodes. I didn't feel like discussing my love life, so we didn't, and Laura simply promised to pray for me.

That night, I tossed and turned. What had happened to my

restful and relaxing vacation? Lake Hideaway was supposed to be my safe haven. Not only had a murder mystery found me, but my love life had also gotten a lot more complicated.

I considered Cal's visit. I hadn't realized I'd needed to hear what he'd had to say, even if it didn't change anything. Was Laura right? Did Cal still love me but didn't want to interfere in my relationship with Hamlet? She seemed convinced she knew the answer to my feelings about Hamlet versus Cal, but it wasn't that simple to me.

Until recently, Hamlet had been a model boyfriend, and now, other than wavering about his career choice, he wasn't doing anything wrong. He still called. He'd come to visit when Laura had invited him. We had good chemistry.

But something Hamlet had said to me last winter came to mind. When he'd seen me in Latte Conspiracies for the first time in years, he'd wanted to know if Cal and I were engaged. When Hamlet found out Cal and I weren't, he'd made the statement that he would've already sealed the deal. In retrospect, it was a pretty cocky thing for him to say, and he'd later apologized for trying to steal me away from Cal.

But when my relationship with Cal crumbled, Hamlet was there waiting.

Now here we were, several months into our relationship, and Hamlet had yet to seal the deal. I didn't want a quick engagement, but the comment bothered me. What if Hamlet really was flaking on me because he wasn't as devoted as I'd thought? Or was I just into Hamlet because I'd thought he was really into me?

I considered my reluctance to follow Hamlet. Was I gravitating toward Cal simply because he'd made a permanent home in Wildcat Springs?

I closed my eyes and thought back to the sermon the pastor had preached at boat church. With the chaos of the explosion, I hadn't reflected on the message like I should've. What was the scripture he'd referenced about trusting God? I got up and rooted through my suitcase for the bulletin. There it was—Psalm 62:8.

Trust in him at all times, you people; pour out your hearts to him, for God is our refuge.

That was the key wasn't it? God was my refuge, and I needed to trust him. "Lord, be my refuge, and forgive me for looking for refuge in anything but you," I whispered. "I trust you to show me your will." Peace washed over me as I shut my eyes and drifted to sleep.

Buzzzz. Buzzzz.

My phone vibrated on the nightstand and beckoned me from a dreamless sleep. Yawning, I answered.

"Is this Georgia?" a vaguely familiar female voice asked.

"Yes." There was such a long pause that I regretted answering the phone without looking at the number. Was this a prank call? "Hello?"

"Sorry. This is Clover—from the ice cream truck. I apologize for bothering you so late, but I *really* need to talk to you."

My grogginess took a hike. "What's going on?" I sat up and turned on a light.

"I just heard my ex-boyfriend Craig Sutcliffe was arrested for Aaron Lehman's murder, and the stress of it all caused him to have a heart attack."

"I know."

"I'm totally and completely sure he didn't do it."

I blinked my grainy eyes. "And you know this because . . . ?"

"I was staked out in front of his house the night Aaron was murdered."

CHAPTER NINETEEN

The crazy just . . . kept . . . coming. For a half second, I wasn't sure I wanted to hear what Clover might say. But who was I kidding?

I was dying to know.

"Why were you on a stakeout?" I asked.

She heaved a sigh. "Back when Craig and I were dating, I talked him into adopting a cat from the shelter where we volunteered. He needed a buddy to greet him when he came home from work, so he adopted Freddie. I thought Freddie was going to be a house cat, but Craig kicked him out. The poor kitty roams around his neighborhood and gets one meal a day. Craig says Freddie controls the rodent population. But Freddie needs human contact. He's a people-cat. I can't stand the thought of him living outside—especially in the winter." She sniffed. "When Craig broke things off, I *tried* to convince him to let me have Freddie, but he refused . . . just to get back at me."

"For what?" I wanted to know if Clover would tell me the truth.

"He was mad because I sold the diamond in a pendant he

gave me, but I didn't have a choice. I was behind on payments for my ice cream truck, and there was no way I was going to ask him to help me financially. Besides, once you give a gift, you lose the right to say how someone uses it."

"That's very pragmatic." At least she hadn't lied to me.

"I thought so, and Craig doesn't get what it's like to worry about money."

I wasn't sure that was true.

"Anyways, Freddie was *my* buddy, and he never took to Craig. I tried adopting another cat, but Peppermint is super fickle."

I had a pretty good idea where Clover was going with this story—at least I hoped I did. "That must be difficult."

"You have no idea. So I finally decided it was time for Operation Rescue Feline. Thursday night, I picked some scraps off a rotisserie chicken, borrowed my friend's gray sedan so I'd be inconspicuous, and parked down the street from Craig's house. I figured Freddie would wander by, and I'd lure him in. Craig would assume Freddie got squished by a car or eaten by a coyote. Plus, we've been broken up long enough that I figured Craig wouldn't suspect me."

In spite of my groggy state, I found this story completely captivating. "Did you apprehend Freddie?"

"Yes. He came padding by at about six the next morning. I was getting so sleepy, I almost missed him, but once I opened the door and offered the chicken, he hopped in and ate like he was starving. He was purring, so I know he was glad to see me."

"I bet." Fresh chicken would make any cat happy.

"As soon as I nabbed him, I took off. Feel free to judge. But I'm telling you, Craig got home around eight-thirty that evening and didn't leave all night. I suppose he could've killed Aaron early on Friday morning after I left, but that doesn't seem likely because he wouldn't have been able to dump Aaron's body in the dark."

She had a point. The sun would've risen around 6:15, and Craig had come home in daylight the evening before. "Doesn't he live on a channel?"

"Yes, but from where I was parked, I could also see his boat, if that's what you mean."

"It is. What about his neighbors' boats?"

"He didn't take those either—no one did."

I squeezed the bridge of my nose. "I don't suppose you've told Detective McCloud about this."

"And admit I'm a kittynapper? No way. That's why I called you."

"All right." I had a feeling Detective McCloud might be willing to overlook a wrong turn in a cat custody battle if it meant solving a homicide, so I'd do my best to convince Clover to talk to him. "Is there somewhere we could meet in the morning?"

Estelle's Estaminet, in spite of its ridiculously fancy name, was just a greasy spoon in Hidden Shores where Clover had agreed to meet me the morning after her phone call.

A tinny bell announced my arrival in the stuffy diner. There was a long, chipped counter with barstools and booths lining the windows. The air conditioner couldn't keep up on the humid morning, and the smell of fried food hung in the thick air. I was certain I'd have to go for a nice, long swim later to get rid of the grease that was sure to cling to my hair. The diner's one redeeming quality was its lake view—if you didn't mind looking across the road and between two brick buildings.

Clover waited in a corner booth, and she wore a red bandana

knotted into a headband. I slid into the duct taped vinyl seat across from her.

"Do you think I'll go to jail?" She yanked a tea bag out of the mug and plopped it on a saucer next to a lemon.

"I doubt it, but you need to contact Detective McCloud now instead of waiting until he finds out on his own."

She gazed out the window toward the lake. "I loved Craig, you know. His parents spoiled him, and he has a terrible temper. But he could be thoughtful and kind. The whole time we dated, I only wanted him to reach his potential."

"Is that why you wrote an obituary for him?"

Her cheeks reddened, and she couldn't meet my eyes. "Who told you about that?"

"Nora Sutcliffe."

"Figures. To her, I was just gold-digging, Crazy Clover." She strangled the lemon over her mug. "At least I cared about her brother making something of his life. I was trying to get him to think about how he wants to be remembered, which he should've already done since he's like twelve years older than me. I wrote an obituary for myself, and my friend Penny did too." She tossed the poor little lemon back onto the saucer. "We didn't think it was weird."

"But a birthday gift?"

"What do you get a rich guy who can buy himself whatever he wants?" She met my eyes.

"Fair enough. Have you heard anything about his condition?"

"No. I hope he's okay." She rubbed her temples. "And even though he can be a complete jerk, I can't let him go to prison for Aaron's murder."

"Then make the call." I slid a scrap of paper with Detective McCloud's number across the table.

She tapped on her phone and waited. "This is Clover Calloway. I'd like to talk to you about Craig Sutcliffe as soon as possible. I have some information that might exonerate him." She disconnected and set the phone on the table.

"You did the right thing," I said.

She fiddled with a saltshaker. "I know."

A few seconds ticked by, and it seemed like a good time to change the subject. "I stopped at Lakeview Park to get ice cream on Monday a little past noon, but you weren't there."

"I had to make a supply run." She set the shaker aside. "That morning was a lot busier than I'd expected, and I had to call my friend Penny to come and get me. Then her VW bus broke down, so I was late getting back."

The VW bus was consistent with what the chocolate loving mother in the park had reported seeing. Clover might be eccentric, but my gut screamed that her worst criminal act was kittynapping. She'd also scored points with me for her honesty about selling the diamond in her pendant. Her community involvement made her a great source, and she was certainly willing to help, but before I got too comfortable with her, I wanted to study her reaction to the BlackBlaze incident.

"I had some excitement that day after I left the park," I said. "Someone driving a BlackBlaze 8200 gave me a scare while I was on my friend's WaveRunner." I watched her expressions as I told her about the chase, and her shock seemed genuine.

"That's really scary." Then concern disappeared from her face, and she bristled. "But a minute ago, you were asking where I was yesterday afternoon. Do you think I could've been driving since I wasn't selling ice cream?"

"It crossed my mind, but your story checks out. A woman at the park saw you leave in a VW bus, and as far as I can see, you have zero motive for killing Aaron. What reason could you have for warning me away from this case?"

"Thanks. I think." She sipped her tea. "I suppose the cops are saying Craig tried to run you down."

"Detective McCloud connected him to this incident through Danielle DuPont who owns a BlackBlaze and lives with her boyfriend who's—"

"Craig's neighbor."

"Right." I opened the picture I'd taken of the BlackBlaze owners. "But if Craig didn't kill Aaron, then he wouldn't have scared me." I turned the phone toward her. "These are the other people who've purchased that model from Thurston's Marina. Anyone look familiar?"

Clover leaned forward and studied the list. "No. I don't know any of those people—other than Danielle."

I opened the picture of Valerie Hudson on my phone and turned it toward Clover. "Do you recognize her?"

She straightened, and her eyes lit up. "That's the chick from the country club who came to Lachlan's asking for Aaron last winter. What's her name?"

"Valerie Hudson."

"Have you figured out why she was at Lachlan's asking for help?"

"She may've been in trouble because of drugs, but I don't know for sure."

Clover traced her finger around the edge of her saucer. "I see."

I tucked my phone away and glanced around the diner, but no one seemed to be paying attention to us—not even the lone server. "Speaking of drugs. Remember how you told me you thought Aaron was selling them at a party recently?"

"Yes."

"Are you *sure* it was Aaron? Sheila Thurston showed me an Instagram post of Dee and Aaron in Chicago the weekend before last."

"I'm totally certain. The party was on a Sunday night because a lot of people were staying around all week for the July fourth holiday." She picked up her phone. "Maybe Dee and Aaron went to Chicago earlier in the weekend, came home, and then she shared the photo." She turned the device so I could see. "The picture *was* posted Sunday night, but Dee included #later-gram, so we know she posted later than it was taken."

I compressed my lips. "I didn't see the hashtag when Sheila showed me."

"She's old." Clover shrugged. "I bet she doesn't know what it means."

The hashtag was pretty self-explanatory. But whether Sheila was trying to be deceitful or was simply clueless, it was fair to conclude that Clover had told me the truth about seeing Aaron at the party.

"I was at Arlene's Café and Variety Store the other day when I ran into an Amish girl named Lizzie. She had the word *hope* tattooed on her arm," I said. "She's Aaron's cousin, and I think she's the girl you saw talking to him."

Clover coughed. "An Amish girl. With a tattoo. You've *got* to be joking."

"Nope. Lizzie denied being at the party, but her nervous behavior said otherwise."

"Now I'm super intrigued. I had no idea Aaron had Amish relatives." She reached into her pocket and tossed a few bills on the table. "Tell you what. I'm not selling ice cream until I make rounds tonight, so other than talking to Detective McCloud at some point, I've got all day to help you get to the bottom of this case."

It couldn't hurt to try talking to Lizzie again, and the service at this place was terrible. "I'm in the mood for some cinnamon rolls from Arlene's. Want to join me?"

She practically leaped out of the booth. "You betcha."

The middle-aged Amish woman working behind the bakery case at Arlene's Café and Variety Store adjusted her glasses and gaped at Clover's denim underwear-like shorts as we approached.

Did she own any other kind? I wasn't trying to be critical. I legitimately wondered, because that was all I'd ever seen her wear.

I smiled at the Amish lady. "Is Liz—"

"Do you know where we could find Lizzie?" Clover glanced around the store. "I've been dying to raise chickens, and she promised she'd help me get going. There's nothing better for breakfast than farm-fresh eggs."

"How do you know Lizzie?" To say the woman eyed Clover suspiciously would be an understatement of epic proportions.

"I was in here last week, and we got to chatting." Clover hooked her thumb in her belt loop. "Are you Arlene?"

"Yes."

"Well, Arlene, I need to talk to Lizzie about the chickens as soon as I can. Will you please help?"

Arlene stiffened. "I didn't know Lizzie was in the chicken business."

Clover's eyes widened. "Ohmygoodness. Do I have the wrong person? I could've *sworn* the girl working told me her name was Lizzie."

"Lizzie works here." Arlene narrowed her eyes. "I've never heard her talk about a chicken business."

"For reals? You should ask her. I bet she'd tell you. She sure gave me an earful. I got so excited, I went home and binged on YouTube videos about raising baby chicks. I'm all about YouTubing stuff out." She hesitated. "Wait. I'm sooo sorry. Do you know what YouTube is?"

"I've heard of it." Arlene didn't flinch.

I choked back a laugh. "Could I buy some cinnamon pecan

rolls? Three pans. I'm going to put a couple in the freezer." I didn't want to be judged for my pastry consumption.

Arlene looked at me as if she were just realizing I was there. "Certainly." Her severe expression relaxed.

"My boyfriend and I were here earlier this week, and I bought some. They're already gone." For the record, Laura had done some serious damage as well, so I didn't feel too guilty.

Arlene beamed. "I'm glad you enjoyed them." She turned around to get a sack. "I baked them myself."

"Keep distracting her," Clover mouthed as she entered the variety store and darted down an aisle with thread and other sewing notions. Before I knew it, she'd slipped through a door with an *Employees Only* sign.

My heart somersaulted. *Sweet baby chickens in a barnyard.* What was she doing?

"How many pans of rolls do you have to make every day?" I blurted and gave myself a D- for sounding natural, but that was no surprise since I'd cornered the market on awkwardness years ago.

Arlene totaled my purchase and didn't seem to notice I was having a moment. "Twenty pecan and twenty maple glaze. We make cookies and pies too." She motioned toward the bakery case.

"Now that you mention pies, I'm not going to be back in this area for a while, so if I'm stocking my freezer with rolls, I might as well add some dessert. I'm a terrible cook. My specialty is microwave popcorn. My poor mom tried to teach me to cook, and I had to participate in 4-H, but I couldn't get into it. I was more into following my daddy around our farm, but that's how I became a farmer, so I guess it all worked out in the end."

"God has a way of doing that, doesn't he?" She smiled.

"Yes, ma'am." I studied the case and tugged my braid. "I'll take one of each of the apple crumb, cherry, and apricot pies. My friends in my Bible study group love pie, so I'll be prepared next time I host."

Arlene opened the case. "Apple crumb is our best seller." She turned around and put it in a box.

I glanced toward the employee doorway. If Clover didn't get out here soon, I'd go broke stocking up on baked goods.

Arlene boxed two more pies, and I was almost finished paying when Clover darted back into the store. She moseyed over to the candy bins, shoved a scoopful of gummy bears into a plastic bag, and strolled over to us as I gathered my purchases.

"I love gummies." She dropped the bag onto the counter.

"That's nice." Arlene weighed Clover's candy. "I'll have to tell Lizzie you were here. What's your name?"

"Clover Calloway." She held out the money. "You have a great day." After Arlene gave her the change, Clover smiled and sauntered outside.

"I'll enjoy the pies and rolls." I gripped the plastic bag, made a quick exit, and jumped into my truck. "What in the Sam Hill were you doing back there in the employees only area?" I started the truck and cranked the air conditioning.

She held up her phone that had a picture of an address on a pay stub. "Finding out where Lizzie Zook lives."

"Oh." It was virtually impossible to be mad at Clover after she'd made such a valuable discovery. "Nice work."

"I know."

I tapped my truck's navigation screen. "What's the address?" We entered it and headed north on the county road in front of the store. "What possessed you to make up that story about chickens?"

"I figure a lot of Amish people raise chickens. It sounded legit to me."

"Arlene didn't buy it."

"Maybe. But she wasn't going to let us talk to Lizzie at all if we told her why we were really there." She opened her bag of gummy bears. "Do you seriously never bend the truth when you're investigating?"

"I try not to."

"Just so you know, I *have* always wanted to raise chickens, and I watched a YouTube video—once." She held out the bag. "Want some?"

I took a small handful, payment for her earlier stunt. "What's our plan for approaching Lizzie? She already didn't want to talk about Aaron." I followed the navigation system's instructions, turned left, and bit a strawberry cub.

She nibbled the head off a green gummy bear. "I'm sticking with the chicken story."

"Lizzie doesn't sell chickens."

"She doesn't know that we don't know."

"Fine." I popped the remaining candy in my mouth and slowed as the computerized voice announced our destination was ahead on the right. I swallowed. "Since I already spooked her, I'll stay in the truck."

"Good call." Clover unbuckled her seatbelt. "I was just going to tell you to do that."

I turned into the gravel drive. A two-story white house was surrounded by several barns and a small cottage that I figured was the *dawdi haus*. Horses frolicked in a pasture behind the house, and a chicken coop stood near a large wooden barn. A garden twice the size of mine took up nearly the entire side yard next to the house, and colorful dresses and shirts waved on a clothesline.

I opened my window, and a gust of cool wind rushed in. As I shut off the truck, Clover hopped out and trotted toward the front door. While she waited on the porch, I checked my phone for messages, but movement near the *dawdi haus* caused me to look up.

A very pregnant Amish woman emerged from the house with

a basket. She headed toward the garden, but when she saw my truck, she froze, then approached hesitantly. "May I help you?" Her voice trembled, but she smiled as if she were trying to play it cool.

I stifled a gasp as she drew closer.

It was Valerie Hudson.

CHAPTER TWENTY

Though Valerie's beautiful face was makeup free, and she wore a traditional Amish dress, there was no mistaking her identity. But I needed to stop staring because the last thing I wanted was to scare her.

If only I could relay that message to Clover through telepathy.

I realized Valerie was waiting for an answer. "My friend and I are looking for Lizzie." I motioned toward Clover who was still waiting on the main house's porch. Her back was to us, and I hoped she wouldn't hear us over the wind.

Dark clouds gathered, announcing an impending storm.

Valerie's shoulders relaxed, and she rested a hand on her baby bump. "Liz went to Shipshewana with a friend for the day."

She glanced toward Clover who was cupping her hands around her face and peering through a window.

Merciful heavens.

"Tell your friend the rest of her family is gone too." She set the basket at her feet and rested a hand on her lower back. "Can I give Liz a message?"

"We heard about her cousin Aaron's murder, and we stopped by to give our condolences."

The color drained from Valerie's face. "I'm sure she'd appreciate that."

I brushed a stray hair out of my eyes as the sun vanished behind a wall of ominous clouds. "Did you know Aaron?" I wanted to see what she'd say, though I felt awful for freaking out a pregnant woman.

"Only by sight." Valerie grimaced.

"Ma'am, are you okay?" I peeked at Clover, and she was peeping in another window.

"My little boy may be making an appearance before too much longer." She picked up the basket. "My midwife tells me I've been having Braxton Hicks contractions for a while now, but these feel stronger. The green beans will have to wait." She glanced at the horizon. "Looks like it's going to rain anyway."

"Can I make a call for you?"

"We have a phone for emergencies. Thank you, though." She went back into the house, and the door's lock clicked.

I shut my truck window as the clouds let loose a torrent of rain. Clover scurried toward me and practically dove inside.

"I'm so bummed." She huffed and fastened her seatbelt. "Wait." She leaned forward and looked out the water-spotted window. "The *dawdi haus*."

"I already checked." I put the truck in gear. "Lizzie wasn't there." My gut screamed Valerie's safety could depend on my discretion. Even though I didn't believe Clover killed Aaron, I still wasn't sure how much to trust her.

"Shoot." Clover ran her fingers through her damp hair.

I flicked on the headlights and pulled onto the road. "Sometimes you hit dead ends when it comes to investigating."

"I suppose." She propped her elbow on the door and rested her head on her fist. "There's something else that's bugging me."

"What?"

"Sheila Thurston."

"How so?"

"I've worked with her at the animal shelter, and she's not a Clover Calloway fan. I'm not sure why. I never did anything to her. Did you tell Sheila that I was the one who saw Aaron at the party on Sunday night?"

"Yes."

"Maybe Sheila *does* know what #latergram means and showed you Dee's picture to discredit or frame me," she said.

Sheila *had* called Clover a money grubber, but that wasn't worth repeating. "Why would Sheila frame you?"

"Because she killed Aaron—or knows who did and is trying to protect that person. Sheila asked you to look into the case, right?"

"Yes, because Detective McCloud questioned her son about his meeting with Aaron Lehman, and at first, she wasn't aware Keith had a solid alibi," I said. "How'd you know?"

"I overheard Sheila tell someone when we were at the animal shelter," Clover said. "What if she asked you to investigate just so she could keep tabs on the case?"

I gripped the steering wheel and considered Clover's theory. "As far as I can see, Sheila doesn't have a motive. Thurston's is thriving compared to Sutcliffe Marina."

"Unless she was afraid if Aaron took over, Sutcliffe would give her business more competition," Clover said.

It was a stretch—but I supposed it was possible. "Sheila could've seen me leave on Laura's WaveRunner, and she could've easily gotten her hands on a BlackBlaze. What if Keith was cooperative and showed me the list of BlackBlaze owners because he suspects his mom?" I shook my head. "I just can't picture Sheila driving a BlackBlaze like a maniac."

Clover snickered. "I know, right? But. I *have* seen her ride a Harley."

My eyes widened. "Seriously?"

"She rode motorcycles for years with her husband, so maybe she does have a wild side."

"Now that you mention it, I've seen a motorcycle in her garage and driveway, but it never in a million years occurred to me it was hers."

"I've got an idea," Clover said. "Take a right at the next crossroad."

"Where're we going?" I turned and drove over a hill, leaving my stomach behind.

"You'll see. Stay on this road."

As the rain subsided, Clover directed me to a double-wide mobile home with faded blue siding resting in a small lot surrounded by a cornfield. A 1980s style Mustang was parked in the gravel driveway under a tulip tree.

"I'll do the talking." She hopped out of my truck. "Sam's shy around people he doesn't know."

"Am I allowed to go to the door with you, boss?"

"So you *can* do sarcasm."

"I'm an expert in my head."

"Permission granted." She slammed the door and trotted toward the house.

I pocketed my keys and followed her onto the weathered wood deck. The front door was open, so she rapped on the glass storm door. "Sam, it's Clover. Open up."

A ferocious bark sounded inside the house, and a German shepherd thundered toward us.

I stepped back and gripped the deck's railing, unsure the flimsy door would save us from Guard Dog.

"Hi, sweet Tessie," Clover said. "Is your daddy home?"

Sweet Tessie?

The dog pressed her enormous paws against the glass and whined. With an open bag of potato chips in hand, a gangly young man emerged from the kitchen. He wore cargo shorts and a plaid, button-down shirt. His sandy hair was cut in a modern mohawk, but the short hair remaining on the sides of his head gave the edgy style a softer look.

"Hey, CC." He held open the door and glanced at me. "What's going on?"

"I'm investigating a murder. This is Georgia, and she's helping me."

I was helping *her*? Seriously? As I hesitated on the porch, I literally bit my tongue. I was about a half second from letting the sarcasm in my head take a flying leap out of my mouth.

Clover wrapped her arms around Tessie, who responded by licking Clover's cheek. "She's harmless and my favorite doggie in the whole, wide world."

Sam eyed me. "Tess won't hurt you. Come on in." He held out the bag of chips. "Want some?"

"No thank you." I stepped into the 1990's country style living room, and Clover and I perched on opposite ends of the blue and white checkered couch. Tessie sprawled on Clover's feet, and Sam dropped into a burgundy recliner next to an oak end table.

"I'm looking for Aaron Lehman's killer," Clover said.

"Why?" Sam tossed a chip in his mouth.

"Because I might want to be a detective."

"Last week you wanted to sell your ice cream truck and buy a food truck."

"I'm evolving." She shrugged. "I might do both."

Sam looked at me. "She's fickle. Drove her parents crazy when she was a kid. Still does, even though she's on her own." He popped a handful of chips in his mouth.

He didn't seem that shy to me, and I wondered about the nature of their relationship, but I bit my tongue again. I wasn't sure how much longer I'd be able to keep still, questioning what we were doing here.

"Sam used to work at Thurston's Marina servicing boats," Clover said. "He just started working at Sutcliffe."

Now we were getting somewhere. Maybe I *was* the one helping Clover.

"I need you to be super straight with me." Clover leaned forward, resting her elbows on her knees. "Why'd you quit Thurston's to go to Sutcliffe?"

"Craig Sutcliffe offered me more money." Sam looked at Clover as if she'd sprouted a second head. "You got a problem with me working for your ex-boyfriend?" He crunched the chips.

"Not necessarily," she said.

"How long have you been at Sutcliffe?" I didn't care what Clover had said. I wasn't good at keeping a sock in it and needed to know if Sam was the lousy mechanic Craig had hired to cut corners.

"Two weeks. About a month ago, I was at the bar in Lachlan's. Craig saw me, and we got to talking. He'd heard about my reputation with boats and said he'd had to fire a mechanic and was looking for a new guy. I thought it sounded like a good opportunity, so I jumped. Gave my two-week's notice at Thurston's."

"Was Keith Thurston the one spreading rumors about Sutcliffe?" Clover stroked Tessie's head.

"Thing is, they weren't rumors. I saw the damage firsthand when I was working at Thurston's and people brought in their boats after they'd been at Sutcliffe," Sam said. "Keith was right to warn people, but Craig was trying to fix the problems he'd created. When he took over for his pop, he tried to cut corners and hired some bozo for a mechanic. That bit him in the backside, and he was looking for someone to come in and fix the problem. I fit the bill. We were well on our way to doing that because I checked everything myself."

"Sam can fix anything," Clover said.

"How would you describe Craig's relationship with Aaron Lehman?" I asked.

"My feeling was Aaron wasn't Craig's favorite person, but Craig needed help and Aaron had offered it. Plus, Aaron saw an opportunity to create a job for himself. He was one of those real smooth guys who could sell you the shirt off your back."

I considered the text message Keith had shown me. "Were Aaron and Craig planning to bribe Keith?"

Sam brushed his hand against his shorts. "Not that I know of. But I did overhear Craig and Aaron talking one day, and they were going to propose a possible merger with Thurston's."

CHAPTER TWENTY-ONE

Clover and I looked at each other with wide eyes. I considered what Sam had told us. Did Sheila kill Aaron because she opposed a merger? Did she think it would ruin her husband's legacy? But as long as Craig was still alive, it could still happen, and Keith had seemed to have no idea what Craig and Aaron were planning.

So how could Sheila have known?

"When you worked at Thurston's, how much was Sheila involved?" I asked Sam.

"Not at all. Keith took over before his dad died, and a few months ago, Keith bought out his mom's share. It's *all* his." Sam leaned forward. "I overheard the receptionist say even his wife doesn't have a claim because she had to sign a prenup. I guess she's always threatening to divorce Keith but has never followed through."

No wonder Keith had seemed so nonchalant when she'd threatened him after the bomb-pop blow up.

"I thought the Thurstons and Sutcliffes didn't get along," Clover said. "So why would they merge companies?"

"Because they like the out-of-town owners of Hideaway Marina even less, and they'd both like nothing more than to put that place out of business." He stood and rolled up his chip bag. "Sorry, ladies. I've got to get back to work. My lunch break is almost over."

I smothered a sigh. It sounded like our Sheila lead was a dead end.

As soon as Clover and I left Sam's house, Detective McCloud called and wanted to see her immediately. I dropped her off at her tiny house, which was located around the corner from her friend's mobile home. She headed to Webster City, and I returned to Laura's and nuked some leftover pizza.

When I finished eating, I took Gus for a walk to the beach since he'd been cooped up in his crate. The storm had moved on, leaving behind a chill because the sun remained hidden. I mulled over everything Clover and I had learned, and with Sheila appearing innocent, my mind turned to Valerie Hudson.

Now that I knew she lived nearby instead of in a Texas rehab facility, she wasn't exonerated from involvement in Aaron's murder. Valerie must've needed a place to stay while she was pregnant, and Aaron had connected her to his Amish relatives. But why live like the Amish and let everyone believe she was in rehab instead of admitting she was pregnant? Was she hiding? Or had she decided to become Amish?

Given her nervous behavior, hiding seemed more likely.

I sat on the damp wooden bench and stared out at the gray, churning water while Gus sniffed and grazed in the grass. A fishing boat puttered from the channel into the lake.

What if Valerie's baby was Aaron's, and he'd hidden her to keep the secret from Dee? Had Dee found out and killed him?

Knowing he had another child when they'd struggled to have one could've enraged her.

Dee certainly had a temper like her brother Craig, and she would've been able to frame her brother easily. I'd seen her in action when she'd threatened Alexa and then nearly taken Lachlan's arm off after he'd tried to pat her belly.

But the major problem with both Dee and Valerie as murder suspects was that I couldn't picture a pregnant woman dragging a dead body around and dumping it into the lake—without help.

When the sun ducked behind a gray cloud, warning me that we were in for round two of the rain, Gus and I headed back to Laura's. I sure hoped we were getting this much precipitation at home because my corn and soybeans could use it.

As we approached Laura's driveway, Sheila stood next to her mailbox.

"We got that nice soaking rain I was talking about. Cooled everything off." She withdrew her mail and glanced at the sky. "Looks like we're not done yet."

"Maybe it'll cool people off too."

"I sure hope so." She shuffled through her stack of envelopes. "There is one bit of good news. Dee Lehman's in labor. My daughter-in-love is her midwife, so I'm keeping Julian."

I froze. "I thought Rachel was a nurse." No, I'd heard Alexa the waitress call her a nurse, and Dee hadn't corrected her.

"Certified nurse-midwife."

My mind flitted to Don and Caterina Sutcliffe's conversation at the country club. "Does Rachel work in a birthing center?"

"No. She goes to women's homes. With her background, she helps a lot of Amish ladies." Sheila looked up from her mail and eyed me as if she expected a comment.

"Good for her." I guided Gus inside and unhooked his leash. I couldn't shake the feeling I was missing something important. There'd been too many mentions of midwives as of late.

Dee's parents didn't want their daughter to use a midwife. Today, Valerie Hudson mentioned needing to contact her midwife. Now, I'd learned Rachel Thurston—former Amish girl, cousin to Aaron Lehman, and sister to Moses Zook—was a midwife.

I'd assumed Rachel was a nurse without question. What else had I missed—or taken at face value?

I squeezed my eyes shut, reviewed my assumptions, and a crazy idea slammed into me with the force of a speeding grain truck.

Dee Lehman wasn't really pregnant.

CHAPTER TWENTY-TWO

"Am I crazy, Gus? Could Dee be faking her pregnancy? After all, she *was* an aspiring actress."

My dog gazed at me as if he wanted to help with an answer but found the matter as puzzling as I did.

I considered Dee's odd behavior. She'd threatened to pound Alexa at Lachlan's Lighthouse, traveled out of state with her due date close, insisted on a home birth.

And she'd completely freaked out when Lachlan had tried to touch her belly.

All of those actions had other reasonable explanations, and why would Dee and Aaron go to the trouble to convince people she was pregnant with a miracle baby when they could simply tell everyone they planned to adopt?

But what if adoption *wasn't* simple?

Aaron's felony drug conviction would at the very least complicate the process, and even parents with spotless records might never have a birth mother choose them. What if last winter, Valerie went to Aaron because she was pregnant, and he saw an opportunity to guarantee a child for his wife?

Valerie could go live with his Amish relatives. Dee could pretend to be pregnant. If his cousin Rachel was willing to deliver Valerie's baby in secret and falsify a birth certificate, then potentially, she could register Dee and Aaron as the baby's parents.

Or Aaron truly was the baby's father.

Whatever had happened, it couldn't be a coincidence that Valerie and Dee were in labor with boys at the same time—and were both using a midwife.

Another thought hit me. Was Valerie even aware of the arrangement or were Dee and Rachel planning to tell Valerie her baby died? Or worse, Dee and Rachel were planning to kill Valerie and claim she died during a home birth gone wrong.

I removed my phone and called Laura, but when she didn't answer, I sent a text.

Call me. ASAP!!!

I should tell Detective McCloud, but what if I was wrong? My theory was certainly crazy, but I'd had wild ideas before. My phone buzzed with Laura's answer.

In an important meeting. Will call later.

"Ughh, Gus! Why?" I typed a response.

Valerie Hudson is pregnant and hiding out in Amish country with Aaron's cousins. Dee may be faking her pregnancy and planning to take Valerie's child. Not sure if Valerie is aware. Or if Aaron was the father.

Surely that would get an answer, but agonizing minutes

ticked by with no response. Had she turned off her phone? "Come on, Laura. Answer!"

I didn't have a choice. I dialed Detective McCloud, but he didn't pick up. Maybe he was still talking to Clover. As his voicemail kicked on, I stepped into my flip-flops and shut Gus into his crate.

"This is Georgia Winston, and I've stumbled upon some information that you might find helpful, and I'm not sure if it has anything to do with Aaron Lehman's murder, but it may." Ignoring Gus's angry woofs, I charged out the front door. "If I'm not making sense, I'm sorry, but please . . . call me as soon as you can."

I disconnected as I hopped into my truck. I had to check on Valerie Hudson.

While I drove, another thunderstorm popped up, and lightning flashed on the horizon. My truck's windshield wipers kicked at high speed, struggling to keep up with the deluge. Water flooded a small dip in the road, but I plowed through with a *swoosh*. When I approached the Zook farm and turned into the driveway, I spotted Rachel Thurston's gray minivan with the stick-family decal plastered to the rear window.

My stomach churned. Now what? I checked for text messages—nothing.

Grabbing Clover's empty gummy-bear bag, I set my jaw. It was time for a Clover move. I shoved my phone in the plastic bag, tucked it into my pocket, and hopped out of my truck. I ran toward the *dawdi haus*. Plastering myself against the siding, I peeked into a window. Just an empty kitchen.

I turned the corner and peered through another window on the back of the house, only to find a vacant bedroom.

Thunder rumbled, and my T-shirt and denim capri pants clung to my body. I swiped water from my face and raced to the next window.

My heart thudded as I took in the scene. Valerie lay on the bed, and Dee sat beside her, holding her hand. Rachel was nowhere to be seen.

Valerie's face twisted, and Dee straightened and appeared to be coaching her through the contraction. My eyes fell on Dee's flat tummy. A silicone prosthetic belly lay in a blob on a chair in the corner.

If Valerie knew Dee wasn't pregnant, she was in on the scheme, which meant her life wasn't in danger—at least not from Dee and Rachel. Earlier, Valerie had seemed spooked about something involving Aaron.

Rachel entered the room, examined Valerie, and said something to the women.

I moved away from the window and stood pressed against the house, where the soffit protected me from the worst of the rain. A few feet to my left, a waterfall streamed from overflowing gutters and splattered into a mud patch.

I forced myself to review facts and reconsider my assumptions. Valerie, who'd lost her family, had turned to Aaron for help about six months ago. She must've been distraught over her pregnancy, and I'd been wondering if it was because he was the father.

But what if he wasn't?

Thunder crashed, and wind assaulted the maple tree behind the house. A branch cracked and tumbled into the yard.

Could Valerie have gone into hiding because the baby's father didn't know about the pregnancy—and she didn't want him to find out? Aaron and Dee illegally adopting her baby would solve a problem for all of them.

They'd be parents.

Valerie and her baby would be safe.

Except the father must've figured out the plan. Perhaps he'd even killed Aaron while trying to figure out where Valerie and her unborn child were hiding. Whoever this man was, he must've had a lot to lose if the affair were discovered.

My stomach dropped. Valerie frequented the country club. What if she'd had an affair with Governor Milton? Hadn't Caterina Sutcliffe said she didn't want her husband playing golf with "that man" because of his past affair?

I pulled my phone from my pocket, removed it from the baggie, and searched the governor's name along with the word *affair*.

Nothing except some shady political blogs dedicated to smearing every move the governor made. Not a single reputable news site had reported the governor having an affair. There was one other major problem.

The governor had been a widower for ten years.

I mentally replayed the Sutcliffes' conversation and then stilled. Don Sutcliffe wasn't just golfing with Governor Milton.

He was also going to play with Byron Collins.

CHAPTER TWENTY-THREE

Caterina Sutcliffe must've been talking about Mayor Collins instead of Governor Milton. If Byron had an affair with Valerie and discovered she was pregnant, maybe he threatened her and the baby. She fled to protect their lives. Had Byron suspected Aaron knew where Valerie was hiding and killed him while trying to get information?

With shaking fingers, I tapped Detective McCloud's number. "Please pick up. Please, please, please," I whispered.

Once again, his voicemail kicked on, and I focused on being more specific with this message now that I'd confirmed my theory. "This is Georgia Winston. Dee Lehman has been faking her pregnancy, and Valerie Hudson is pregnant and hiding out with Aaron Lehman's Amish relatives. I think Dee plans to adopt Valerie's baby because Valerie Hudson and her baby could be in danger from the baby's father." I needed Detective McCloud to believe me and didn't want to accuse the mayor without more proof.

As I disconnected, the saturated yard squished.

"What's going on?"

With a flipping heart, I whirled around and came face to face with a drenched Clover. I pressed my hand to my chest and clenched my teeth. "What're you doing here?"

"I left my phone in your truck, and when I tracked it, I realized you came back here without me." She put her hands on her hips. "Why?"

I didn't owe her an explanation but motioned toward the window. "Take a quick peek—and pay close attention to who's on the bed and look at the chair in the corner."

Clover stepped around me, pressed herself up against the siding, and glanced in. When she turned back, her hand was clasped to her mouth. She dropped her hand. "Ohmygoodness. Dee's been faking her pregnancy, and Valerie Hudson isn't in rehab. This is totally insane. Why would Valerie hide her pregnancy?"

"I think Byron Collins is the baby's father—but I'm not certain. Maybe he threatened her if she carried the baby to term." I explained to Clover the reason I thought Aaron and Dee had wanted to adopt Valerie's baby after they discovered she wanted to hide her pregnancy from Byron.

"So Byron killed Aaron while trying to figure out where Valerie was hiding."

"Exactly."

Clover nodded, eyes wide. "Now what?"

"We have to get to Detective McCloud. Valerie and the baby's lives could be in danger. I've tried calling him, but his phone goes to voicemail. My friend Laura could help, but she's in a meeting and isn't answering."

A steady rain continued, and a gust of wind sprayed us with cold drops.

Clover rubbed her bare arms. "Let's get to the sheriff's department."

We hurried around the house. "How'd it go with Detective McCloud?" I whispered.

"I'm not sure what he thought since he plays close to the vest. He's not going to arrest me for catnapping Freddie. But." She stuck out her lip. "I have to return him to Craig."

"Maybe Craig will work out custody since you're saving him from a murder charge."

"I hope."

We made sure the driveway was clear before darting to our vehicles. Clover hopped in a green VW Beetle, and I followed her as we raced to Webster City.

By the time we reached the sheriff's department on the outskirts of Webster City, the rain had subsided, and the clouds had begun to scatter. Still drenched from our spying expedition, Clover and I splashed through standing water in the parking lot and into the building that was attached to the county jail.

At the front desk window, a pudgy man eyed us with amusement as we dripped on the white tile. "Looks like the rain got the better of you. Can I help you ladies?"

"Is Detective McCloud here?" I glanced behind the man but didn't spot the detective among the sea of desks. But there wasn't much else to see. Beige walls. Glass block lined the wood door next to the reception window. A chipped blue laminate counter protruded from the wall.

"It's urgent." Clover looked around.

"Sorry, but he left."

Clover and I exchanged glances. "Do you know when he'll be back?"

"Tomorra mornin'. He went to be with his daughter at the

Hideaway Amateur Ski Competition. Sure is proud of that girl." He glanced at his cellphone. "Thought the storms might cause a cancellation, but it's gonna clear up and be a real pretty evening."

"Is there anyone—?"

"We'll catch him tomorrow." Clover clawed my arm and dragged me toward the door. "Thank you," she shouted.

"What was that all about?" I muttered as we exited the building.

"We know where to find Detective McCloud."

"But another detective might've been able to help us."

"Detective Foster is the mayor's high school buddy. Now, I'm not saying Foster's in on it or a bad guy, but McCloud is at least fair enough to listen to us without bias. Foster's a good old boy." She unlocked her car. "Why don't you tell me how you knew to go back to the Zook farm?"

Busted.

"I talked to Valerie earlier, and she thought she was going to have to call her midwife. When I got back to Laura's, Sheila told me her daughter-in-law Rachel, who used to be Amish, was Dee's midwife—and that Dee was in labor. It seemed like too big of a coincidence. Plus, I thought about Dee's strange behavior like almost getting in a fight, traveling out of town close to her due date, and freaking out about someone trying to touch her belly."

"Why didn't you tell me you found Valerie?"

"Because I don't know you that well, and Valerie's hiding for a good reason." I put my hands on my hips. "Are we going to keep discussing this, or are we going to find Detective McCloud?"

"Fine. People can watch the ski competition from the shore in Lakeview Park or from their boats. With all the traffic, we can buzz across the lake faster than we can wind around it to the park. You allowed to drive your friend's boat?"

"I sure am."

On the way to Laura's house, I tried calling again, but her phone went straight to voicemail. As soon as I parked in her driveway, I sent a text.

Going to find Detective McCloud at ski competition. Call me!

Clover hopped out of her car and jogged around the house toward Laura's boat. Gus howled when I entered the house to get the boat key hanging near the back door.

"Sorry, boy." I raced out of the house and across the soggy back yard, where Clover was tugging off the cover.

She hefted the heavy material into the grass, and we hopped aboard. I lifted the engine cover, sniffed for fumes, and having learned my lesson from Byron's explosion, let the blower run.

"What're you doing?" Clover put her hands on her hips. "Let's go!"

I shoved my phone in the cupholder. "Practicing boat safety, so we don't . . ." I whipped around as another piece fell into place. "Call your boyfriend."

"My what now?"

"Sam. I have a question about Mayor Collins's boat."

"Gotcha. We're just friends, by the way." She tapped her phone and waited. "Hey. Georgia wants to talk to you. You're on speaker."

"You heard about Mayor Collins's boat exploding, right?" I asked.

"Yep," Sam said.

"Mayor Collins told me he had his boat serviced at Sutcliffe Marina on Saturday before it blew on Sunday due to a leaky fuel hose."

Sam chuckled. "That may be what he *says*, but I checked the line myself, and there wasn't a thing wrong with it on Saturday when it left our shop. He can sue if he wants, but I'd swear to that in court."

"Thanks for your help," I said.

Clover's eyes widened as she disconnected. "Do you think Mayor Collins tampered with his boat's fuel line, so it would explode?"

"Possibly. If he had Aaron's body on the boat and wanted to get rid of evidence." I cranked the engine.

She untied the boat and pushed us away from the seawall. "How could he be sure that would happen?"

"He couldn't, but he was willing to take a risk so that the explosion would look accidental. He certainly increased his chances by not running the blower."

"Wouldn't his wife have smelled gasoline if it was leaking?"

"Minnie has allergies, and she was pretty plugged up the night before."

Traveling the channel at idle speed was excruciating, and as soon as we passed the buoy line, I shot across the lake at full speed. Since it was a weekday, there was very little traffic on the lake, and the relatively smooth water made it easy to glide toward Smith Bay.

A crowd had gathered in Lakeview Park, though the skiing competition had yet to begin. I buzzed back around the peninsula to Calloway Cove and slowed the boat as we approached the public piers that were nearly full. Clover was missing a fantastic business opportunity. "I'm keeping you from selling ice cream."

"This is more important."

There was no mistaking the strain in her voice.

Spotting a single space in the shade of a massive cottonwood, I eased the boat up to the dock, and Clover caught a metal pole.

We secured the boat, hopped off, and jogged uphill and through the trees toward the action in the park.

Shading my eyes, I scanned the crowd. Metal bleachers full of spectators faced the bay. Other people sat in colorful lawn chairs and sprawled on towels. Competitors waited in boats offshore, and a blue and white striped tent was arranged to the north of the bleachers.

Where was Detective McCloud?

"Welcome to the twenty-sixth annual Hideaway Amateur Ski Competition sponsored by Thurston's Marina and Lachlan's Lighthouse," a deep male voice boomed through the P.A. system. "Please direct your attention to the American flag as Hidden Shores High School sophomore Mia McCloud sings 'The Star-Spangled Banner.'"

Mia McCloud. Surely, she was the detective's daughter.

Clover and I stopped, pressed our hands to our hearts, and faced the flag in the center of the park while the teenage girl in a white sundress and red sandals sang the national anthem from the judge's platform near the tent. While she sang, I tried to spot her dad, but I couldn't see him. I nudged Clover. "Do you see Detective McCloud?" I asked when Mia finished the song.

Clover squinted at the mass of humanity. "No. I wish we had binoculars, so I could see who's in the boats. I'll search the bleachers. You take the tent. Call if you find him." She darted away before I could protest.

A boat motor revved as the first slalom competitor skimmed across Smith Bay. He cut across the wake while water sprayed around him. I'd never been able to slalom with that much confidence.

Hoping for a message from Laura or the detective, I reached into my pocket for my phone, but it wasn't there.

"Uhhggg." I must've left it in the boat's cupholder.

Racing back through the crowd, I headed toward the piers as the sun vanished behind the clouds.

"Georgia!" Tommy waved as he and Zenith approached from the parking lot.

Oh boy. I considered his friendship with the mayor. How would Tommy react when he learned his buddy had killed Aaron?

"If I'd have known you were coming, I'd have told you to tag along," he said. "Zenith loves this competition."

I motioned toward the piers. "I left my phone in Laura's boat. I'll be right back and join you."

"I'll find a spot for us." He adjusted the blanket on his arm and turned toward the crowd.

Just then, I remembered something Laura had told me to ask him about Byron. "Hey, Tommy?"

"Yeah?" He turned as Zenith tugged him toward the crowd.

"Is Byron Collins mechanically inclined?"

He chortled. "No way. Minnie's the one who does all that work. Her dad was a boat mechanic—taught her everything he knew."

My stomach plummeted.

"Hurry, daddy!" Zenith jumped up and down.

"Why?" he asked.

"Just wondering." I tried to sound casual. "I'll be right back. Better get Zenith a seat before she yanks your arm off."

They hurried away, and I jogged downhill through the trees as my mind spun. If Minnie had tampered with her boat's fuel line, had she killed Aaron because she wanted to find Valerie—and the baby?

But why?

When I stepped onto the dock and approached Laura's boat, I sighed with relief when I spotted my phone resting in the cupholder next to the driver's seat.

At least there were still honest people left in the world. Or it might've been because I'd snagged the last pier space and no one else had walked by. Hoping for a message from Laura or Detective McCloud, I squatted and grabbed my phone out of the boat, but neither one had responded.

The dock creaked. As I stood, a blow from behind sent me tumbling into the boat.

CHAPTER TWENTY-FOUR

A rms flailing, I pitched over the driver's seat. I landed face
up, and my head conked against the boat's deck.

Stars flickered through my vision, and my breath vanished.

Someone was scurrying around. Doing what?

I sucked in air and tried to move, but my long legs tangled
awkwardly in the narrow walkway to the bow.

Lord, help!

The boat's engine roared to life, and I patted the deck in
search of my phone while the boat reversed and turned. My
fingers closed around the device as my vision cleared, and I
untwisted my legs.

"I'll take that." Minnie Collins bent down from the driver's
seat, yanked my phone out of my hand, and tossed it overboard.
Then, she pulled back on the throttle, and the boat zoomed across
the lake.

Ignoring my throbbing head, I focused on sitting up because I
had to fight. But with what? The boat didn't offer many possibilities, and Zenith's pink lifejacket wouldn't do much damage.

A spray can of sunscreen that I'd used earlier this week was within my reach in a cupholder at the foot of the seat. I could squirt the sunblock in her face and try to get control of the boat. Keeping my eyes on Minnie, I scooted until my body blocked the can. "Why are you doing this?" I yelled over the engine.

She looked at me with disdain. "Damage control. I was in a meeting with Laura and saw your texts while she was in the restroom."

My heart dropped as I grasped the container. "And you deleted them."

"Obviously." She sneered. "She probably wonders why I cut our meeting short."

Minnie's sleeveless blouse displayed toned arms strong enough to have dragged Aaron's body around, and my foggy brain spun with possibilities. "Does Byron know?"

"No. And he never will." She fixed her gaze on the lake.

I pulled out the can and sprayed it in her face. She shrieked, and I used the seat to hoist myself up on shaky legs while she swiped her eyes.

Before I could pounce, she stopped the boat in the middle of the lake and leveled a gun at me. "It's your turn to drive." Her eyes watered.

I froze. The weekday boat traffic was light, and not a single watercraft was close enough for someone to see her weapon. Her gun hadn't been part of my plan, and I weighed my escape options.

If I jumped overboard and tried to swim to shore, she could shoot me in the water, and I'd make her job of disposing of my body a lot easier. At least by driving, I'd have control of the boat, and I could use that to my advantage when my brain felt less fuzzy. I slid behind the wheel. "Where are we going?" I couldn't keep my voice from trembling.

Keeping the gun pointed at me, Minnie perched on the seat beside me. "Little Hideaway."

I kneaded the steering wheel. That tiny lake with only a handful of cottages was connected to the main lake by a winding channel.

In other words, unless I figured out how to escape, it was the perfect place for disposing of my body.

Or not.

"Dumping Aaron Lehman's body in the lake didn't work," I shouted as I guided the boat across the lake. "Some poor soul will eventually find me when I gas up in the warm water and float to the surface."

"Not if I bury you in the woods behind my mom's cabin instead."

She made the statement as matter-of-factly as if she'd just offered me a bowl of ice cream.

"Well, that's a game changer." As soon as the comment slipped out, I wanted to shove it back in my mouth. *Really, Georgia? A game changer?*

"I like games."

"Why'd you kill Aaron?" I asked.

"It's complicated."

"It's simple. You hit him in the head, killed him, and dumped his body in the lake."

"You're a real gem, aren't you?"

"My boyfriend thinks so." Where was a sock when I needed it?

Minnie wiped her red eyes. "Valerie Hudson is pregnant with my husband's child, and she's willing to do whatever it takes to keep the baby from Byron and me."

So she *was* going to talk. "Why?" Not that Valerie hadn't made a good call. Had Tommy seriously never noticed Minnie was unhinged?

Minnie adjusted her grip on the gun. "Because Byron and I planned to fight for at least partial custody of her child, and with her history of drug abuse, we could've gotten full custody."

Their money would've helped too.

"When Byron found out she was pregnant, he asked if she'd share custody since our lives have felt so empty after our daughter Avery died." She swallowed. "Valerie told him she'd consider the arrangement."

"And you were fine with the idea of raising another woman's child?" I found that hard to believe.

"Yes. I'm a good mother, and I can't have any more children." She sniffed. "Their affair was done, and neither Byron nor I have a great track record when it comes to marital faithfulness."

I remembered Don Sutcliffe mentioning the wife who'd cheated first.

"Then Valerie texted Byron and told him she'd had a miscarriage. When he went to check on her, she was gone. We heard the trauma caused her to relapse, so she went to a long-term rehab facility in Texas."

"You didn't buy that story."

"Byron did, but he's always been gullible. The story seemed too convenient to me."

"How'd you figure out she wasn't in rehab?" I asked.

"I found the name of the facility where she'd been a patient before, did some digging, and confirmed she wasn't there."

"Isn't that information confidential?"

"Money opens mouths, and I have plenty." She waved a hand. "I also heard a rumor that she'd turned to Aaron Lehman for help before she left Hidden Shores."

I slowed for a wave, but water still sprayed the windshield. "So you confronted Aaron to figure out where Valerie was hiding?"

"Aaron loved to jog the trail after work, so I docked our boat at Lakeview Park and waited for him. The plan was to wave my gun around and get him to spill his guts."

"But he didn't?"

"He refused to tell me where Valerie was hiding, wrestled the gun out of my hand, and tried to shoot *me*." She sounded legitimately offended.

I didn't blame him.

"I hadn't loaded the gun because I never intended to kill him. But I learned my lesson—and I'm definitely planning to get rid of you."

I gritted my teeth. "Then what happened?"

"Once he realized the gun was worthless, he turned to run, but he tripped and fell on the trail. At that point, I couldn't let him get away, so I smashed a large rock into the side of his head. That did him in. I dragged him onto my boat, took him and the rock out to Smith Bay and—well—you know the rest. Turn down this channel." She pointed to her right and pulled Zenith's lifejacket onto her lap to cover the gun.

I slowed the boat and followed the narrow waterway. Houses dotted each side, but not a soul was outside. Where were all the retirees and vacationers? We floated under a bridge as cars drove overhead, and the marsh spread before us with a watery path winding through the cattails and lily pads. Ahead, a bass boat crept toward us.

"Smile and nod when he passes," Minnie demanded. "Or I'll kill him too."

I complied, and the man in a wide-brimmed hat and khaki vest hardly appeared to notice us. "You blew up your own boat to hide the evidence, didn't you?" I asked as soon as we were a safe distance from the fisherman.

"I sure did. I'd heard about the problems at Sutcliffe Marina and figured we could easily blame them for a faulty fuel line, so I tampered with the new one they put in on Saturday. Byron never ran the blower like he should've, so I wasn't too worried about my plan working."

I kept my hands at ten and two and my eyes fixed on the water. "And you were the one who chased me with the BlackBlaze?"

"Yep."

"Where'd you get it?"

"Our friends Buck and Nancy Templeton own one. I was at their house feeding their cat while they're on vacation, and I spotted you riding around Calloway Cove. I thought it'd be fun to give you a little scare."

"Did you suspect Valerie was hiding with the Amish after Byron arranged a meeting with Moses Zook?"

"It crossed my mind. I couldn't ask too many questions, so I quietly investigated. I hadn't gotten very far until today, when you handed me the answers I was looking for." She smiled. "Serendipity."

The marsh disappeared, and trees lined each side of the channel. "What're you going to do about Valerie, Rachel, and Dee?"

"Let them carry out their plan, and when the law catches up to them, Byron and I will get custody of the baby. We'll just prove his paternity."

I set my jaw. The channel's mouth widened, and Little Hideaway beckoned, its placid waters surrounded by trees. I increased the boat's speed.

"No, no, no. Idle speed on this lake."

I slowed. But this was my chance.

She pointed. "Head north."

Please God, help someone notice. I pulled back on the throttle, and the boat rocketed forward.

"Idle!" Minnie lunged for the throttle, and I shot upward,

knocking into her. Her arm flew outward, and she lost her grip on the gun.

It thumped onto the deck. I dove for the weapon, but she grasped my braid. My fingers closed around the gun, and as I rose up bucking against her, my heart skittered.

Our boat careened toward the shoreline. Keeping a grasp on my braid, Minnie jerked the wheel with her free hand, and the boat whipped left. I lost my balance, tumbled sideways, and the gun slipped from my fingers as she slowed the boat.

I flailed my elbows and connected with her nose, cartilage crackling. She roared, and her grip loosened as the boat's path wavered again and glided to a stop, the engine glugging. The gun slid closer, and I locked my grip around it.

As I straightened, Minnie clawed my wrist and slammed it against the edge of the windshield. Pain shot through my arm, but I held on to the weapon and thrust my other fist toward her midsection.

I missed, and she banged my wrist against the windshield again. This time, I couldn't hold on, and the gun flipped out of my hand and splashed into the water.

Blood dripping from her nose, she swore, and her hands flew at my neck. Throwing all my weight forward, I shoved her off balance. She tumbled into the back seat but popped up. As she charged toward me, I leaped aside and used her momentum to shove her overboard.

Cursing, she splashed into the water, surfaced, and flailed toward the boat.

I dove toward the throttle and yanked it back as I fell into the driver's seat. The boat zoomed forward, but when I glanced over my shoulder, I didn't spot Minnie behind me in the water. I rose out of my seat.

She was clutching the ski platform.

The tiny lake's shoreline loomed, and I jerked right to avoid running aground. Zigzagging at high speed, I yanked the wheel to the left, then right, then left again, my stomach sloshing.

I whipped around, and my shoulders sagged at the sight of Minnie screaming and slapping her arms against the water before she swam toward the shore.

I turned toward the channel leading to the main lake, but when I noticed a man standing on his pier with his hands on his hips, I zipped over and stood as I approached.

"I called the sheriff on you, young lady!" He waved a finger at me. "You got no business driving your boat at that speed on this little lake!" His bushy white eyebrows formed a unibrow as he pointed behind me. The sheriff's boat was speeding across the lake toward us, lights flashing.

"Thank you." Battling a wave of nausea, I reached out and caught his pier.

"Don't sass me, missy!"

"No sassing, sir. You're an answer to prayer."

"Huh?"

I dropped back into the seat. "The mayor's wife just tried to kill me."

CHAPTER TWENTY-FIVE

O nce the deputy reported what I told her, Minnie didn't make it very far before another sheriff's deputy apprehended her limping through the woods surrounding Little Hideaway. Mr. Bushy Brows apologized and provided ice packs for my throbbing wrist and head.

After I gave my statement to Detective McCloud, Laura took me to the emergency room in Webster City. We were in a tiny room with a sliding glass door awaiting the results of my wrist X-ray. As I sprawled on the bed, I prayed it wasn't broken, because that was the last thing this farmer needed. The doctor had already told me I had a mild concussion, and I was certain I'd be very bruised from my tumble into the boat.

Laura, who was sitting in a chair beside the bed, looked up from her phone. "Tommy's on his way. I told him you were fine, but he insists on seeing you with his own eyes."

"That's sweet." I wasn't even being Nice Georgia. I actually meant it.

"It's one of the reasons I love him." Her cheeks turned a little pink. "But he feels partially responsible since he introduced you to Minnie Collins."

"It's not his fault she's crazy," I said.

"He thinks he should've seen the warning signs, but any time she seemed upset, he figured she was still grieving her daughter."

"What were you meeting with Minnie about?"

"She wanted to run for state representative and was asking me to help with her campaign. She had some good ideas. I never would've guessed she has such a dark side." She grew quiet and then held up her phone. "Would you like to call Hamlet? You're welcome to borrow mine."

"I will when I have an accurate report about my injuries." I really wished I could call Cal.

"'Accurate report.' You sound like Hamlet again." She smiled. "That's not a bad thing, though. I enjoyed hanging out with him last Sunday."

"I did too."

"But . . ."

"We're headed in different directions, and I need to figure out what that means."

She quirked an eyebrow. "G, you already know what it means, and I can think of a very handsome detective who will be one happy man when you're finally honest with yourself."

The door slid open, and Tommy burst inside. He held a bouquet in each hand and thrust them toward each of us. "How's your hand?"

I took the assorted pink and white flowers. "Sore." I sniffed the rose in the arrangement. "Thank you."

"They're beautiful, Tom-Tom," Laura said.

Even though Tommy had grown on me, I still had a gag reflex over that nickname.

Laura's phone chimed. "I've got to take this." She slipped out of the room.

"When do you have to head home?" Tommy asked.

"Friday morning. I need to get back to work."

"Don't be a stranger. Laura likes having you around." He looked at his feet, then raised his head. "I've got something I need to say to you." He shifted.

I set my flowers on the bed. "I'm listening."

"I know I'm a little rough around the edges, but ever since God got a hold of me a few years back, I've been different. Finally realized I didn't have what it took to make it without Jesus."

"None of us do," I said.

"You're probably worried about Laura, because I'm pretty good at putting my foot in my mouth, but don't worry." He fingered his chain. "I love her and plan on taking good care of her."

"You'd better." I pointed two fingers at my eyes and then at him. "I'm watching." I tried to keep a straight face but couldn't.

He laughed.

"Good news." Laura rejoined us. "That was Ryan McCloud. He asked me to let you know Minnie confessed to Aaron's murder and to abducting you."

"Thank the Lord."

"I still can't believe she had everybody fooled. She seemed like such a great gal, and she was always so good to Zenith." Tommy ground a fist into his palm. "I feel like such an idiot."

"Same," Laura said. "I've been sick to my stomach all evening."

I looked at Tommy. "Have you heard any updates on Craig's condition?"

"He's gonna be fine. It was a mild heart attack, and Nora says he's vowed to lose weight and make some lifestyle changes."

"What about Rachel, Valerie, and Dee?" I asked Laura.

"The prosecutor will review the evidence. They may face

charges." Laura tucked her hair behind her ear. "I'm not sure what's happening with the baby boy Valerie just had."

I ran my hand over the blanket. "This is one situation where nobody wins."

"No kidding," Tommy said.

I took comfort in knowing that Aaron's family could go through his funeral on Saturday with the knowledge that his killer would be brought to justice.

The next morning, I slept until almost noon since it'd taken a long time for the emergency room doctor to appear and tell me that my wrist wasn't broken and that I should get plenty of rest because of the concussion. Laura was at work, and when I was in her back yard with Gus, Sheila and Pickles emerged from her house.

"Well, you did it," she said. "I knew we could count on you to find Aaron's murderer. I got the scoop this morning when I was having breakfast with my friends at Estelle's."

"I'm sorry about your daughter-in-love."

"Rachel made her choices. We'll see what happens, but Keith told me she's open to seeing a counselor to help their marriage, and she may be willing to give him another chance." She petted her cat. "By the way, I did hear that Valerie is going to keep her baby boy, and Dee's okay with that. Rumor has it, Valerie was never afraid of Byron having partial custody of her son—just Minnie. I also heard Byron's planning to file for divorce."

"That's sad."

"Yes. Yes, it is." She shook her head. "You'll have to visit another time when things aren't so crazy. In spite of everything that happened this week, Hidden Shores really is a nice little town."

Later that day, I was lounging on Laura's screened-in porch when the doorbell rang. Gus woofed, shot to his feet, and led me to the foyer.

Clover stood on the front porch, clutching a brown paper sack to her chest.

"Hey, there. Come on in," I said.

"I brought you a sandwich." She patted Gus's head and held out the sack. "It's a BLAT—bacon, lettuce, avocado, and tomato. If I ever have a food truck, I might put it on the menu."

I took the bag. "Thank you. I'm always happy to be a taste tester."

"I figured."

I should've been offended by that statement, but I couldn't fault her for being observant. "I haven't had lunch, so I'm going to dive right in." I led her to the kitchen and didn't even bother getting a plate for the sandwich. The bacon was perfectly cooked, and she'd included a special sauce on the bread, but since I wasn't exactly Martha Stewart, I couldn't identify the ingredients. I just knew I wanted to keep eating.

"Good news," she said. "Craig is going to let me keep Freddie."

"Do you think Freddie will like being a house cat now that he's experienced roaming free?"

"I'm a good cat mom. He'll live in luxury."

I didn't doubt that one bit.

Clover handed me a napkin. "Yesterday, I freaked out when I couldn't find you and your friend's boat was gone. I finally tracked down Detective McCloud right about the time the call came in about the mayor's wife. How'd you figure out it was her and not her husband?"

I told her about my conversation with Tommy, and between

bites, gave her the story of Minnie abducting me at gun point. When I finished, I pointed at my remaining sandwich piece. "And you should absolutely start a food truck. This is amazing."

She grinned. "We'll see. I might still want to be a detective."

The next afternoon when I arrived at home, Hamlet was waiting on the front porch of my farmhouse. He hopped up and darted across the yard. As soon as I got out of my truck, he embraced me. "How are you feeling?"

"Sore." I'd finally called and told him everything the night before, and I'd had to talk him out of coming to get me.

Gus nudged past me and ran in wild circles around the backyard.

Hamlet took my suitcase from the truck and followed me into my kitchen. "I had some interesting news today." A pained expression settled on his face.

"What's that?" I dropped my keys on the table.

"I got the movie role in Chicago."

"Congratulations! That's great!" I hugged him.

Sadness lingered in his eyes. "But given our earlier conversation I fear it's not so great for *us*."

"Are you moving?"

"Perhaps. There are other great opportunities in Chicago, and I already have friends there." He met my gaze. "I love Wildcat Springs and tried to get into house flipping and renovating, but I missed acting too much."

"I know."

"And I can't ask you to give up your career."

"I could be a teacher." I wasn't sure why I said that when that was the very last thing I'd ever want to do.

"Darling, we both know you're meant to be a farmer—right here."

I swallowed over a gigantic lump in my throat. "Just like we both know you're meant to be an actor—wherever God leads."

His blue-gray eyes welled with tears. "I've thoroughly enjoyed your company, Georgia Rae."

"I enjoyed yours too. Thank you for always being so good to me."

He bent and kissed my forehead. "I'll pray that God will always give you his best."

"I'll do the same for you," I whispered.

And then he left.

A week later, the sadness over my break-up with Hamlet had lessened, and I was certain that we'd made the right decision. I hadn't heard from Cal, but I'd been keeping a pretty low profile.

That evening as I weeded my garden, a warm breeze rustled the cornstalks in the field surrounding my house. In the pond next to my garden, ducks glided across the water.

With a sigh, I brushed dirt from my hands and went to my shed to get my mower. I'd just driven it out, when Cal strolled up my driveway. I shut off the engine and heard him whistling "For the Beauty of the Earth."

My heart flittered when I took in his running shorts and the fitted shirt that clung to his muscular chest. I hoped I looked okay. As I slid off the mower, I tucked a stray hair behind my ear.

"So, today I heard that you had some excitement at the lake last week." His forehead creased with concern. "What happened?"

I filled him in on the story of Minnie abducting me at gunpoint, and the scheme that I'd uncovered.

"Wow." He ran his fingers through his hair. "Are you okay?"

"Yeah. My bruises are looking a little better."

"I'm glad." He glanced around. "Where's Gus?"

"Inside napping. He's not allowed out while I'm mowing."

"That's a good rule."

Why were we acting like a couple of junior high kids at their first dance? I studied my grass-stained tennis shoes. "Hamlet and I broke up," I blurted. I couldn't bring myself to meet Cal's gaze—though I could feel it.

"I see." He edged closer.

"He wants to return to acting—and I don't want to hold him back from going where he needs to be. He's a great guy, but it's not meant to be with us and—"

Cal closed the gap between us and kissed me so hard my head spun.

I gathered the strength to step back. "But what about . . . ?" I couldn't bring myself to finish.

He stroked his thumb against my cheek. "My fear of something happening to you like it did with Mason's wife?"

"Yes."

"Our lives are in God's hands, and I'm not going to let the remote possibility of something happening ruin what we have."

"Are you sure?" I wasn't sure I could endure losing him again.

"Absolutely. I don't want to face life without you. You bring so much joy to my life, and—it hasn't been the same without you. Georgia, I love you with my whole heart."

Tears of joy stung my eyes. "I love you too, and I want to be with you—wherever life takes us." I rested my head against Cal's chest, silently praying for God to help us face the future.

Because that was our only hope.

Don't miss Georgia's next adventure in *Deadly Heartbreak* coming in 2021. Stay in touch by subscribing to my e-mail newsletter, and get the latest on all my new releases.

As a thank you for subscribing, you'll gain access to *Deadly Homestead: A Georgia Rae Winston Mini-Mystery and Other Short Stories.*

If you enjoyed *Deadly Hideaway*, I'd be very grateful if you'd leave a short review to help me spread the word about my novels.

ABOUT THE AUTHOR

Jenni Mansell Photography

Marissa Shrock is a survivor of many awkward blind dates and many years of teaching middle school. Both provide excellent inspiration for her fictional yarns.

Since childhood, she's loved to read a variety of genres, so her own work includes dystopian thrillers and cozy mysteries. She's the author of the Emancipation Warriors Series and the Georgia Rae Winston Mystery Series. Her debut novel, *The First Principle*, was a Carol Award Finalist.

Marissa enjoys playing golf, building elaborate LEGO creations, and traveling to new places. Her home is in Indiana, where she's surrounded by corn and soybean fields. Visit her at www.marissashrock.com.

ALSO BY MARISSA SHROCK

CREDITS

Editing by A Little Red Ink

Cover Art by Seedlings Design Studio

Marketing Copy by JR2 Marketing & Advertising

Cimelia Press Logo by Race Point

Beta Readers: Mary Shrock, Brad Shrock, and Katie Briggs

www.ingramcontent.com/pod-product-compliance
Lightning Source LLC
Chambersburg PA
CBHW072051170626
46813CB00004B/1301